My B.F.F. (Bogus Fake Friend)

Book Seven of the Bex Carter Series

Tiffany Nicole Smith

Contact me. I'd love to hear from you!
authortiffanynicole@gmail.com
Twitter @Tiffany_N_Smith

Cover Designed by

Keri Knutson @ Alchemy Book Covers

My B.F.F. (Bogus Fake Friend)

Book 7 of the Bex Carter Series

by

Tiffany Nicole Smith

Other Books in the Series:

#1 Aunt Jeanie's Revenge

#2 All's Fair in Love and Math

#3 Winter Blunderland

#4 The Great "BOY"cott of

Lincoln Middle

#5 Love, Politics, and Red

Velvet Cupcakes

#6 So Scandalous

Books 1-5 of the Fairylicious

Series

Burkley and the Beasts

Chapter 1

Love-Hate Relationship

#hater

Geraldine Cordelia Ulysses could fit eleven Giant Puffed Marshmallows in her mouth. Pretty impressive, I had to admit, but I was determined to break her record.

"Eight, nine," Geraldine counted eagerly as I stuffed marshmallows in my mouth. Only it came out more like, "Aaaaaa, iiiiiii," because her mouth was still full.

I had just barely gotten the tenth one to fit when my bedroom door flew open. Being a member of a huge crazy family, I had come to expect these rude interruptions because the people I lived with had no concept of privacy. But still, would it kill them to knock?

I expected the intruder to be either my little sister or one of my bratty triplet cousins, but the unwelcomed visitor was much, much worse. The rude privacy-intruding door-flinger was Ava Groves, whom I unaffectionately referred to as the Green-Eyed Monster. I mostly called her that because she had green eyes, and well . . . she was pretty much a monster.

She flicked her long, glossy black hair over her shoulder and looked down on us. "What are you losers doing?"

I tried to think of a quick comeback to her calling us losers, but what could I say?

Geraldine and I must have looked like two silly chipmunks sitting there with our mouths full and cheeks puffed out. I grabbed a paper towel and spit out my marshmallows. "Hey! You can't just burst into someone's room without knocking and insult her. Were you raised in a barn? What are you doing here anyway?"

Ava scowled at me. "Didn't your aunt tell you? We're going shopping for graduation dresses." But her face looked like she was on her way to the dentist to have ten cavities filled.

I guess you could say that Ava and I had a love-hate relationship. She *hated* me, and I *loved* floating in her Jacuzzi. My Aunt Jeanie and Uncle Bob also have a Jacuzzi, but Ava's is the top-of-the-line updated version (it has seventy jets and lights up purple at night!) and the only good thing about being forced to go over to her house.

Unfortunately, Ava's mother and my aunt were besties so they made us hang out even though neither one of us could stand each other. The two of us were about as opposite as swans and orangutans. Ava was as girly-girl as you could get. She was always put together perfectly in the trendiest outfits, makeup that looked professionally done, and every hair always in place. Ava did everything that girly-girls did—cheerleading, ballet classes, manicures, pedicures— you name it. I would be lying if I said she wasn't beautiful (at least on the outside anyway), but on the inside, that girl was something else. Worst of all, she was the perfect example of the girly-girl Aunt Jeanie wanted me to be and my aunt didn't waste an opportunity to let me forget it. I think if given the opportunity, she would trade me for Ava in a hot second.

Me, while I was doing a little better at the girl thing, I didn't consider myself a girly-girl at all. I played every kind of sport (soccer and basketball were my specialties). My makeup regimen consisted of washing my face with plain old soap and water (I hid the fancy facial cleansers Aunt Jeanie bought because they made my face itch), running a brush through my wild mane of bushy red hair, and maybe, just maybe putting on some lip gloss if I felt like it. Anyway, regardless of what anyone said, I liked the way I looked and I had plenty of things to do other than looking in a mirror obsessing over my eyebrows.

Ava had been awful to me since the first grade, and we had nothing in common. We would absolutely never, ever be friends. I wished Aunt Jeanie would just accept that.

Ugh. Shopping with the Groves was the worst thing ever.

Ava smoothed down the sides of her sundress. She wore a cute purple halter dress with a silver chain belt and silver sandals with straps that wrapped around her calves. "Trust me, the last thing I want to do is go on a shopping trip with you," Ava said, sneering. "Especially dressed like that."

I looked down at my school soccer team shirt, ripped jeans, and sneakers. Maybe I wasn't as chic as she was, but I was comfortable. After all, I was hanging out in my own bedroom. I wasn't trying to impress anyone. "Then get out of my room and wait downstairs," I ordered.

Ava put her hands on her waist. "You can't talk to me like that, *Rebecca* Carter!"

I cringed. I hated when she or anyone called me by my full name. Ava knew that good and well and didn't miss an opportunity to throw the name *Rebecca* in my face.

Geraldine stood next to me. "This is Bex's room. She can do whatever she wants in it."

Geraldine and I had met just a while ago, but she had proven herself to be a great friend. She was . . . a little weird, but I liked weird. Geraldine was tall and rail-thin with long, light brown frizzy hair. Her oversized glasses and homemade vests made her a major mean-girl target.

Ava looked appalled that Geraldine was even talking to her. "Who gave you permission to speak to me, freak?"

"Don't talk to her like that!" I shouted. "She's my guest."

"Do something about it," Ava challenged.

If I wanted to, I could have pulverized Ava, but I wasn't that kind of person. I decided to take the high road and hold my tongue.

Geraldine looked back and forth between Ava and me. "Bex isn't afraid of you. She can take you down with her pinkie finger."

Ava looked at Geraldine as if she were the most vile, disgusting thing she had ever seen. "Why is 'it' still speaking to me? Seriously, Bex, all you do is hang out with freaks. You're like a freak magnet!"

I spotted my soccer ball near my desk a few inches from me. I imagined it going upside Ava's head, but still, I did nothing. "Just go away," I muttered.

But she just wouldn't stop. Ava had to keep pushing my buttons. "I mean it—Chirpy, Lily-Rose, Marishca—they're all a bunch of freaks!"

Chirpy, Lily-Rose, and Marishca were my best friends in the whole wide world. We had been friends since the first grade and we'd even given ourselves a name—the Tribe. How dare she insult my besties like that? Before I knew it, my soccer ball was flying across the room and landing square in Ava's chest.

Geraldine pumped her fist in the air. "Yes! Goal!"

I knew I shouldn't have done that, but as I tried to apologize, Ava sent the ball back at me—only her aim was nowhere as good as mine. The ball went off to my left, bounced off the wall, and sent my super-cool one-of-a-kind soccer cleat lamp crashing to the ground.

"Look what you did!" I screamed at Ava. "You're going to buy me another lamp!"

"I'm not buying you anything. You physically assaulted me first! I could sue you!"

Aunt Jeanie and Mrs. Groves appeared in the doorway before Ava and I could continue our argument.

"What on earth is going on?" Aunt Jeanie asked, her gaze moving from the broken lamp to me.

"Ava broke my lamp!"

"She hit me with a soccer ball!" Ava and I shouted at the same time.

I had to get my story out before Ava could tell hers so I kept talking, but that fool kept shouting over me.

Aunt Jeanie clapped her hands. "Hey, hey, hey! Enough! Both of you!"

Ava and I both fell silent. I looked at the ground, fully prepared for my aunt to blame the whole fight on me.

Geraldine headed for the door. "This scene is totally throwing off my chi." Geraldine said a lot of strange things I didn't understand, but I took that to mean that we were stressing her out. "I'll talk to you later, Bex."

I couldn't take my eyes off Ava as Geraldine headed for the door. Ava glared at me and I squinted my eyes, trying to glare harder at her.

"I wish you would just evaporate so I could never see you again," Ava said between clenched teeth.

"Ava," her mother said with a warning tone. "Girls, you know this is perfect timing for what we were just talking about downstairs."

My stomach lurched. Aunt Jeanie and Mrs. Groves getting together to talk about Ava and me was never a good thing. Never!

"What were you talking about?" Ava asked, eyeing her mother.

I braced myself for what they were about to say. Aunt Jeanie put her arms around Ava and me. "We've decided that this nasty little feud has lasted much too long."

Nasty little feud? If Ava's looks could kill, I would totally be a homicide victim. What we had going on was way more than a nasty little feud.

"We'd hoped that you girls would have learned to work things out for yourselves," Aunt Jeanie continued, "but apparently that isn't going to happen."

"Maybe you need a little help from us," Mrs. Groves chirped in. "We've decided to give you an ultimatum. You two have one month to become friends, real friends. Either learn how to get along or you'll be spending your summer at my parents' house. They have a quaint little farm in Alabama. It'll just be you two, Grandpa, Grandma, and all the animals. Once you have to get up at the break of dawn every morning—yes, even on weekends, to milk cows with someone, you've got a best friend for life."

Just the thought of spending my summer on an isolated farm with Ava and her grandparents made me wish I could fulfill Ava's request and evaporate.

"Mom, you have to be kidding. You won't even visit Grandma and Grandpa's farm," Ava said. "I cannot spend my summer there. I'd just die! Die!"

"Then you girls had better get it together. Enough is enough," Mrs. Groves replied sternly. She looked her daughter in the eye. "Mrs. Mahoney and I are tired of playing referee between you two. We spend too much time together for you girls to be at odds all the time. Honestly, it's exhausting."

I was speechless. What was wrong with these two? You can't just force people to be friends. That's not how friendship works. I felt as if I had been set up to complete the impossible. How could I ever be friends with such a horrible person?

"Now," Aunt Jeanie said as if everything was all settled, "let's get to that mall. We have some graduation dresses to buy."

Yes, we were getting ready to graduate from middle school and that was a big deal, but there was no way I could get excited about this shopping trip. The only thing I hated more than Ava G. was shopping with Ava G.

Before we left, I texted Santiago (my BF!) to let him know that I was on my way to The Shopping Trip of Death and if he never heard from me again, that was why. He replied that he wished he could save me, but he knew I was strong enough to survive. Of course there was nothing he could do, but it was nice to have his support. One of the many things I liked about him was that he always made me feel better.

Aside from all that he's absolutely adorable, although I hadn't realized that until recently. It's amazing how you could know someone for years, and then all of a sudden you looked at him in an entirely different way. Santiago had gone from being this cool but sometimes annoying kid to a total cutie with tan skin, dark curly hair, and the cutest dimples. I have always been a sucker for dimples.

Anyway, shopping wasn't my favorite thing to do in the world, but I actually liked shopping with my friends and people who liked me. Shopping with Aunt Jeanie was already tortuous. Adding Ava and her mother to the mix was downright inhumane.

As we walked into the Lincoln Square Mall, I felt as if I were in a game of "One of these things is not like the other. One of these things just doesn't belong." My Aunt Jeanie was a very pretty lady, small and petite with jet black hair that came just past her shoulders and large dark brown eyes. She credited her flawless porcelain skin to her weekly fancy facials. Frankly, I thought the whole facial thing was a racket. Just rub some yogurt or something on your face and be done with it.

Mrs. Groves was a little taller and very, very thin. She always looked as if she had just stepped out of a catalog for expensive clothes. I don't recall a time I had ever not seen her in heels, not even at our annual school picnic. I could swear that she had a live-in professional makeup artist.

Ava G. was obviously her mother's daughter. Besides the gorgeous black hair that contrasted beautifully with her bright green eyes, everything about her was the perfect size, or at least what Aunt Jeanie and most people considered the perfect size. She wasn't too tall or too short. She wasn't too skinny or too big. She had tiny dainty feet— nowhere close to my size tens.

I, on the other hand was the thing that didn't belong. Thick, curly, flaming red hair flowed like a lion's mane down my back. I was taller than all the girls in my school and not exactly what someone would call skinny. I had curves that I was just learning to embrace. I loved my size. Being an athlete, my body type came in handy although Aunt Jeanie didn't see it that way. She has been a lot better about not criticizing me though.

We headed straight for Glittering Goddesses, where my aunt and Mrs. Groves knew all the salespeople by name. They were even good friends with the owner, Ms. Primrose. (Yuck!) I felt the same way about Ms. Primrose as I did about Ava G.

"Hello, ladies," she gushed as we walked in. I was sure she was expecting us. Her large gold accessories jingled noisily as she pulled us all into a hug.

Ms. Primrose was a big-haired blonde who constantly bragged about all the beauty pageants she had won, beginning at the age of two. She was always telling Mrs. Groves how she had missed the boat with Ava and should have had her competing in pageants since birth. She never said anything like that to Aunt Jeanie about me. "Everyone goes through that awkward stage" was the best compliment I had ever gotten from her.

Ms. Primrose clapped her hands. "I've already picked out some dresses I think you girls will like. There's a rack for Ava and a rack for Rebecca."

"Bex," I said, promptly correcting her.

She gave me a tight smile. "Right, Bex." She paused for a moment as if biting her tongue and then finally spit out what she was thinking. "But Rebecca is so classic and feminine. Bex just sounds like—what a truck driver would be called."

I would have loved to be a truck driver at that moment if Ms. Primrose would be a speed bump. Every time I shopped in her store, it seemed that she went out of her way to make me feel small.

"Well, it's my name, not yours, so you don't have to worry about it," I said in my sweetest voice.

"Bex!" Aunt Jeanie snapped. "I'm sorry, Primrose."

"It's all right," she said, giving my aunt a sympathetic glance as if to say *Poor you for having to deal with your burden of a niece.* "Bex's fitting room is over there."

Thankfully Ava's fitting room was down on the other end, so I wouldn't have to see or hear her. I wheeled my rack of hideous fluffy dresses to my assigned room. I could already tell that I would hate every dress Ms. Primrose had picked out for me. The dresses were so awful I thought she had picked them on purpose knowing I would loathe them.

I started to tell Aunt Jeanie this when I pulled a dress from the rack to discover that it was huge. I mean two of me could have fit in that thing. I knew I wasn't skinny, but did Ms. Primrose consider me to be the size of a baby elephant?

"Oh dear," Aunt Jeanie said as she looked through all the dresses. "Primrose, will you come here a second?"

Ms. Primrose pulled herself away from gushing comments about Ava through her fitting room door.

"You're such an easy girl to style. It's like dressing a living doll." (Barf!)

"I haven't seen a dress that hasn't looked spectacular on you." (Gag!)

"Yes, Jeanie?" she asked as she strutted over in her six-inch heels.

"All these dresses are way too big for Bex."

Ms. Primrose looked me up and down. "Are they? Are you sure?"

"Are we sure? Anybody with eyes can be sure!" I snapped.

Aunt Jeanie tapped my arm. I usually wasn't so disrespectful to anyone, especially adults, but I knew this lady was being mean to me on purpose.

Aunt Jeanie smiled at her friend. "I did send you her measurements."

"You did. I'm so sorry. Let me pull some more," Ms. Primrose said quickly.

"Why don't we just let Bex pick out the dresses she'd like to try on?"

Thanks, Aunt Jeanie. It wasn't every day that she backed me up.

"Sure," Ms. Primrose said, looking quite constipated. "You know," she called as I looked around, "Lily-Rose Johnston was just in here this morning and found a gorgeous little dress. She's a friend of yours, right? It's always fun dressing her."

Of course it was because Lily-Rose was tiny like the rest of my friends. The Johnstons were just as uppity as my aunt and Mrs. Groves, so it was no surprise to me that Ms. Primrose liked them.

By then Ava had stepped out in a gold-sequined dress looking absolutely stunning. As usual, the entire staff of Glittering Goddesses had to rush over to admire her perfection. I wondered what that felt like.

Putting Ava out of my mind, I made my way toward an emerald green dress. Green was one of my favorite colors, and people said it looked great on redheads. Aunt Jeanie picked out a few pink and purple tutu-style dresses because she loved dressing me up like a cupcake.

I absolutely refused to try on more than five dresses per shopping trip, so once I had five dresses, I headed for a dressing room.

I tried on the green dress first since there was no way I would be wearing the pink and purple monstrosities, even if they did fit. I could tell from the oohs and aahs coming from the other side of the store that Ava had found another winner.

I looked at myself in the mirror, and well . . . I wasn't sure how to feel. It was a little snug but not in a bad way. The dress was strapless, with a strip of sequins going around the waist. The more I looked at the dress, the more I liked it. It was beautiful, yet simple and I looked so grown up wearing it.

Aunt Jeanie rapped on the door. "Bex, let me see."

I opened the door and braced myself for what she would say.

She gasped as she took me in. I couldn't help but smile.

Aunt Jeanie turned me around so she could look at me from every angle. "Oh, Bex, it fits you perfectly. It's like this dress was made for you."

"Really?"

"Yes! With some gold accessories and the perfect shoes. It has to be a heel, Bex," she added quickly as I made a face. "It's gorgeous."

"Wow. I can't believe I found the perfect dress on the first try."

Aunt Jeanie's smile dropped immediately. "Are you crazy? We're not getting this dress."

Huh? Was *she* crazy?

I was totally confused. "What are you talking about? You just said it was perfect."

"It looks great on you, but this dress is totally inappropriate, especially for a fourteen-year-old, especially for a school function."

You have to be kidding me. "What's wrong with it?"

"It's too tight. Look at your hips. Look at your . . . *boobs*," she said, whispering the last word as she pressed down on my chest area as if she could make them smaller.

"Aunt Jeanie, stop it. I don't like when you say boobs. I'm getting this dress."

"You are not!"

I scowled at her. "I know what you're doing. You just don't want me to look good. Why does Ava get to be the only one who looks beautiful? Why can't I get the one dress that looks right on me?"

"It's the only one you've tried on. Take it off and try on something else."

Why? Why would I do that when I had already found the dress I wanted? After all, the whole purpose of this shopping trip was for me to find a dress I liked and I had.

"No," I said, folding my arms across my chest.

"Bex!"

"If you don't let me get this dress I'm not trying on another one!" I shouted. "I won't!" The buzz of the shop grew a little quieter. Maybe I had been just a tad too loud.

Aunt Jeanie got in my face and gritted her teeth. That's when I knew she meant business. She might be small, but she could be very scary. "You have fifteen minutes to find another dress so we can get out of here before I die of embarrassment. *Fifteen minutes* or you won't live to see high school."

Then she slammed the fitting room door shut and marched off. Since I didn't want to die in the middle of Glittering Goddesses, I chose a plain black dress with absolutely nothing on it. I didn't even try it on.

"Are you sure, dear?" Ms. Primrose asked as I slammed my selection down on the counter. She picked the dress up and looked at it as if it were something I had dragged in off the streets. "We actually only keep this dress in stock in case someone needs something to wear to a funeral."

"Who cares? We're wearing caps and gowns anyway. No one will even see the dress."

Of course Ava couldn't resist butting her nose in my business. "But we're taking the robes off afterward for pictures and when we go out to dinner. Is that really the statement you want to make on our last day of eighth grade?" No, but the statement I really wanted to make would have gotten me grounded for life so I said nothing.

I watched as Ms. Primrose rang up three beautiful dresses for Ava because she couldn't decide on the one she wanted.

"They all look so beautiful, I might wear one before, during, and after the graduation ceremony," Ava announced and everyone laughed.

Not finding the right dress wouldn't have been so bad if Ava hadn't been there to rub it in my face. One of my real friends would have encouraged me or helped me find a dress I liked that Aunt Jeanie would approve of. Ava would never do anything like that for me. She relished the fact that I was miserable. How on earth were we ever going to become friends in a month?

Chapter 2

The Graduation "Committee"

eye roll

Journal Entry #17

Hey, Aunt Alice. You said I could always be honest and straightforward with you, so I'm going to do that right now. I'm kind of getting tired of keeping this journal. I know you said I had to in order to go with you to Australia this summer, but I think it might be a waste of time because I might not end up going anyway. See, Aunt Jeanie wants me to become friends with you-know-who and she might as well be asking

me to climb Mt. Everest. It's looking like you
might be going to Australia without me.

The car ride home from my disastrous shopping trip
wasn't much better than the trip itself. Ava was going on
and on about how she was ruling the Graduation
Committee and had just passed a decree (yes, she actually
said decree) that the graduation colors would be coral and
magenta because those were the favorite colors of Chanel
Featherstone (Ava's famous bubble-headed idol).

Coral was sort of an orangey-pink and magenta was a
purplely-pink and neither of those colors belonged at our
graduation ceremony. As far as I knew, the Graduation
Committee was made up of a team of eighth-graders
working together to choose the décor and songs, as well as
put together a slide show of our class memories that would
play on the big screen during the ceremony. There were no
officers. No one was in charge except for the guiding
teacher, Mrs. Diaz. Everyone was an equal. Still it came as
no surprise to me that Ava was treating this as her personal
party planning committee, putting together the perfect Ava
Groves celebration. It didn't help that the committee was
made up of her friends and people who were afraid to stand

up to her. No one would dare vote against any of her stupid suggestions.

Naturally, my aunt and Mrs. Groves found nothing wrong with this.

"Ava," I said, "don't you think the auditorium should be decorated with the school's colors? That's how it's always been."

She rolled her eyes. "I know that's how it's always been. That's why I'm trying to do something *different*."

"Step out of the box, dear," Mrs. Groves called from the front seat, encouraging her daughter. It was my turn to roll my eyes.

Ava sneered at me. "Stay out of it. If you cared, you would have joined the committee."

"You're right. I think I will. First thing Monday morning."

Ava shook her head furiously. "You can't. It's too late."

"Oh, I'm sure it's not." Aunt Jeanie said. "It'll be just the perfect opportunity for you two to bond."

I smirked at Ava as she slid down in her seat. Aunt Jeanie and Mrs. Groves went on chatting about their summer vacation plans while Ava shot me daggers with her eyes.

"I hate you," she mouthed.

"I hate you more," I mouthed back.

Monday morning I went straight to Mrs. Diaz's classroom to sign up for the committee. I found her on her laptop typing quickly with a very focused look on her face. It seemed as if she was trying to finish something up at the last minute.

"Uh, Mrs. Diaz?"

She looked up, and her messy bun bobbed on her head. "Oh, good morning, Bex. What's up?"

"I wanted to know if I could join the Graduation Ceremony Planning Committee if it wasn't too late."

By the time I had gotten that out, she had gone back to typing. "Sure, Bex. It's not too late." She pointed to a clipboard on the edge of her desk. "Just add your name to the list."

"Cool. Can I sign up my friends Chirpy, Lily-Rose, and Marishca, too?" I figured the more numbers I had on my side, the more I could keep Ava from taking over, so I wanted to add my guy friends, Santiago, Jeeves, and Maverick to the mix too.

"Sure," Mrs. Diaz said absently. "The more the merrier. See you at the next meeting after school today."

"Yes, you will," I said as I scribbled my friends' names down, feeling very pleased with myself. I couldn't wait to see the look on Ava's face at the next committee meeting. Little did she know that her reign of terror was over.

During lunch, I decided to inform my friends of my actions. I was sure they'd be thrilled.

"By the way, we have a Graduation Committee meeting after school today in Mrs. Diaz's room. It's very important that we all be there because Ava G. has gone completely overboard trying to take over."

Everyone stared at me.

"Bex, we're not on the Graduation Committee," Lily-Rose Johnston said, looking at me over the rim of her lavender glasses. Her black hair had been flat-ironed and pulled up into a perfect ponytail. She wore a pretty dainty-looking pink dress that looked stunning against her brown skin.

"Yeah, you all are. I signed us up this morning."

"Bex!" everyone screamed at the table.

I was used to this reaction from them. "Guys, trust me. This is for the good of everyone. Ava's trying to make our ceremony colors coral and magenta. Do you want that? I can only imagine what lame song she picked for our class song. This is our graduation too. We need to have a say. Do you want our last middle school memory to be some Chanel Featherstone-inspired ceremony that only Ava likes? Come on. The meeting won't be any longer than thirty minutes."

"Lily-Rose and I have band practice. The band's going to be playing at the ceremony, and we have a lot of music to learn," Maverick said. Lily-Rose played the violin and Maverick played the drums in our school's music program. They were both really good at their instruments, which helped make them the perfect couple.

Everyone else muttered reluctantly, saying they'd come. I looked at Santiago who had been unusually quiet this whole time. "Santiago?" As a matter of fact, I hadn't spoken to him that entire weekend.

His dark eyes flashed me a worried look. "I can't. After school I have to go right home and . . . help my dad do something."

"Do what?" Chirpy asked.

Santiago took a few seconds to think about it, which led me to believe that he might not have been telling the truth. "Uh, paint some stuff, you know."

The girls and I exchanged confused looks, but I let it go.

"So anyway," I said. "This is great. Operation Save Graduation is underway!"

My friends looked at me frozen and wide-eyed. Chirpy leaned forward. "Bex, enjoy this now because I'm warning you. There will be no more *operations* when we get to high school." She pushed her short brown hair behind one ear and gave me her serious look.

The others nodded in agreement. I didn't get it. They were acting as if I did stuff like that all the time.

"Whatever." I didn't want to think about high school or how things were going to be different so I changed the subject. I told them about the ultimatum my aunt and Mrs. Groves had given Ava and me.

Marishca looked as if she were about to cry. "I'm so sorry, Bex. You are going to have a meezerable summer on zat farm," she said in her Russian accent. The others looked as if they felt sorry for me also.

"Too bad," Chirpy said. "That trip to Australia sounded like it was going to be awesome." They all shook their heads solemnly.

My friends knew me well. They knew the sky would fall and crash into the sea before Ava and I would ever get along.

Our Graduation Committee meeting started off horribly. Mrs. Diaz went into her office which was connected to the classroom to make a phone call. Ava G. planted herself in front of the classroom as if she were in charge. The other Avas, Ava T. and Ava M. (yes, there were more of them), who were almost as bad as Ava G., stood beside her.

It only took me a few moments to realize that this was not a committee but a kingdom, and Ava G. had appointed herself queen.

"I'm so glad everyone could make it today. The other Avas and I got together yesterday and made some finalizations on our ceremony." She unfolded a sheet of pink paper and read from it. "The colors will be coral and magenta," she said, shooting me a dirty look.

Everyone groaned, but no one said anything. Chirpy raised her hand, but Ava ignored it. I grabbed Chirpy's arm and yanked it down. "Just say what you have to say. You don't need her permission. She's not in charge."

Chirpy nodded and stood up. "Excuse me, Ava. I think we should have a discussion about the colors. By the groaning, I can tell most of us aren't happy with them and frankly, those colors would be horrible for our ceremony."

Ava narrowed her eyes at Chirpy. "Sit down, *Beatrice*."

Ouch. Chirpy's real name was Beatrice. She was named after her grandmother and hated her real name probably more than I hated mine. I couldn't blame her. Beatrice was pretty bad. We started calling her Chirpy when we were little because she had a large nose that looked like a bird's beak. Of course, her nose and nickname were things she embraced or we would have never called her that.

Chirpy stood up tall. "I prefer to be called Chirpy. I think you know that since it's what I've gone by since the first grade."

Ava wrinkled her little button nose at Chirpy. "Oh, have you? See, I thought it was Twerpy. I was trying to address you with a little dignity."

"Let's get back to the point," I said, sensing Chirpy was about to lose it. "Those colors are awful. You guys can't just decide things on your own and then come back and tell us what they are. That's not the purpose of a committee. We're supposed to decide things together."

Ava started to say something, but I cut her off. "All in favor of the colors magenta and coral, raise your hand."

Only three hands went up—you guessed it, the three Avas. Ava glared at a group of girls in the corner of the room. They slunk down in their seats looking ashamed.

"You guys said you liked those colors," Ava said accusingly.

One girl shrugged. "I'm sorry, but they're not right for this. They'll clash with the auditorium. The seats and the curtains are dark green." As soon as she was done talking she looked away from Ava as if she were about to be punished.

"Right. Good point," I said. "I was thinking that we should just go with our school colors, gold and green."

Ava made a gagging sound. "Très tacky. But I wouldn't expect anything more from you, Bex."

Lily-Rose spoke up. "I think that's a great idea, Bex. All in favor of green and gold, raise your hands." Every hand in the room went up except for the Avas.

"Awesome," said a kid named Kenny. "Now let's talk about a song. We should make a list of suggestions, listen to the songs before the next meeting, and then take a vote. It should be a song that means something to us."

Ava pouted. "But I already picked a song."

"I don't think the theme song of Chanel Featherstone's reality show is the best we can do," Kenny said. "Throw out suggestions and I'll write them on the board."

Ava looked appalled as Kenny grabbed a dry erase marker and started writing while kids shouted out song names. She and the other Avas took their seats once they realized they weren't running things anymore.

After a few moments Mrs. Diaz came back into the room. "Well, it's nice to hear lively discussion going on. It's usually so quiet in here."

Right, because it was Ava doing all the talking and everyone else just listening. That was going to change.

By the end of the meeting, everyone looked ten times happier. On the way out, the Avas brushed past me on purpose, almost knocking me over, but that was okay. Ava G. always threw tantrums when she didn't get her way. I heard her mutter, "Ruining everything," under her breath to the other girls as they walked by.

I said good-bye to my friends as they set off to walk home and headed for the front of the school to wait for Aunt Jeanie. I sat on the top step of the school's entrance thinking about a great song that would sum up our eighth-grade year.

"Hurry up, Mom!" a voice shouted from behind me. Ava G. was yelling into her cell phone. She hung up and stood on the other side of the staircase glaring at me. I tried my best to ignore her.

"You just had to ruin everything," she said after a minute. "You weren't even interested in the committee before."

"That's because I thought it was a group of kids making wonderful choices for the good of our class ceremony, not a bunch of scared kids sitting back and watching a power-hungry banshee make all the decisions. And I didn't ruin anything, I made it better. You were turning our ceremony into your own personal party."

"Why can't you just stay out of my life? Don't even act like you know me next year."

"Ah, but we're supposed to be becoming best friends," I said sarcastically.

Ava groaned and plopped down on the step as if she had forgotten about that. "You know what I was supposed to be doing this summer? Going to Camp Pointe. The best dance camp in the country. All the top dancers have gone there. You have to send in an audition video to be accepted. I've tried three years in a row. I finally made it and now it's all ruined."

"Well, I was supposed to be going on an awesome trip to Australia with my aunt and now I'm going to be stuck on some boring farm with you and people I don't even know."

Ava opened her mouth to say something when Aunt Jeanie's SUV pulled up. Unfortunately, sitting in the front seat was Mrs. Groves, which meant that we would be going home together.

Ava looked up at the sky. "O . . . M . . .G!" she shrieked as if her entire world had just come to an end. So dramatic.

"I'm sitting behind my Aunt Jeanie," I said. That was the best spot for the air conditioning and it was a super hot day.

"No, I am," Ava said, probably for no other reason than to argue with me.

We made a mad dash for the car, but I was faster than she was. Ava caught up to me as I fumbled to open the door. She tried to shove me to the side and I shoved her back. This went on for about ten seconds, but I was victorious and climbed inside first.

"Well," Mrs. Groves said as Ava and I settled in. "I take it the bonding hasn't been going too well. Jeanie, we'd better take these girls shopping for some overalls and work boots."

She was probably right.

Chapter 3

Boy Problems

—feeling confused ☹

Journal Entry #18

It was foolish of me to think having a boyfriend would end my boy problems. Things were going great with Santiago and then he just started acting super weird all of a sudden and I don't know what's wrong with him. I can't help but to think it's me. Whatever the problem is, I just wish he would come right out and say it.

One minute he's the sweetest guy ever and the next he's acting as if he hardly knows me. Can somebody please explain boys to me? They're like some mysterious creatures I'll never understand.

The next day at lunch, I filled Santiago in on what had happened during the Graduation Committee meeting.

"That's great, Bex," he said. "Leave it to you to change things around." He sounded like he meant what he said, but he looked sad.

"What's wrong? I called you and texted you last night, but you didn't answer."

"Oh, I was busy helping my dad cut the yard."

"I thought you were painting."

His eyes opened wide. "Oh, yeah, yeah," he said quickly. "We painted too."

"You couldn't stop for a second to just send me a text?"

"I'm sorry," he said looking down at his taco. "Gotta love Taco Tuesdays, huh? I'm going to miss that next year." He was obviously trying to change the subject, but before I could say anything, Jeeves dropped down at the table looking severely distressed.

"Jeeves, vat's vong?" Marishca asked.

"What's wrong is that I'm a big, giant loser!" Jeeves wailed. Were these kids trying to win an Academy Award around here? In his tuxedo and slicked-back hair, Jeeves did look like someone who stood on stage giving awards away. He wore a tuxedo to school every day because he wanted to be an orchestra conductor when he grew up and his father had taught him that he should dress for the job he wanted.

Maverick patted his best friend on the back. "Hey, Jeeves, be nice to yourself, man," he said, sounding like our guidance counselor.

Jeeves took out a small black comb and combed his hair back in place. "I *am* a loser. What else do you call a kid who can't pass the eighth grade?"

"What are you talking about?" I asked.

"Mr. Chin just told me that I'm failing English. I need that class to graduate with you guys. If I don't pass, I can take it over the summer and still go to high school, but I won't be able to take part in the ceremony. My mom and dad were all excited about seeing me walk across the stage. They actually talked to each other for the first time in months."

Poor Jeeves.

"School's almost over. Why is Mr. Chin just telling you about this now?" Chirpy asked, looking a little angry.

Jeeves shrugged. "I don't know. He might have told me a few months ago . . . and had a conference with my mom about it . . . and given me a progress report that said 'in danger of failing' . . . but that's beside the point!"

Lily-Rose handed him a napkin to wipe his tears. "There are still a few weeks left, so you have time. How bad are your grades?"

"He gave me this huge project to complete in two weeks and I have to get at least a ninety-eight on our final to just barely scrape by. You know how Mr. Chin's projects are. They're killer. I'm doomed."

I'd never had Mr. Chin. I had another teacher for English, but Mr. Chin had the reputation of being the hardest teacher in the school. I heard kids complaining about the work he assigned all the time, and I was glad I didn't have him.

"Don't worry, Jeeves. We'll all help you," I reassured him.

"Yeah," Maverick said. "Santiago is acing that class."

"Oh, sure. Don't worry man, I got you," he said, but he didn't seem to be paying much attention to the conversation.

One thing I loved about Santiago was how smart he was. He wasn't just book smart, but he was always coming up with some kind of business or some way to make money. Come to think of it . . . he hadn't been doing that lately. Hmm . . .

The others continued to comfort Jeeves while I turned to Santiago. "We still playing basketball later?"

"Huh? That was today?"

"Yes, we play basketball every Tuesday." It was a standing date. On Tuesdays Santiago would come over to Aunt Jeanie's, we would play basketball, and Sophia would make us milkshakes and fries. I actually looked forward to Tuesdays.

"Oh, I'm sorry, but I can't today. My mom said I have to go right home," he said.

"Okay," I said, not wanting to pry. There was no mistaking it. Something was going on with Santiago. He was definitely avoiding me. He was my first boyfriend, so maybe I was doing this girlfriend thing all wrong. I racked my brain trying to figure out what mistakes I could have been making, but nothing came to mind.

Since Santiago had ditched me, I invited the girls over after school to hang out and talk about songs for the graduation ceremony.

"It's Tuesday," Chirpy said. "Aren't you and Santiago supposed to be playing basketball?"

"Yes," Marishca added. "Nozing says romance like beating your boyfriend in basketball and then rubbing it in his face."

"Hey, we have fun, even though I do always win. Santiago canceled. Guys, I think something's going on with him."

"He has been quiet lately," Lily-Rose noted. "And he's usually loud. Very, very loud."

"I feel like he's avoiding me. He doesn't want to hang out. He doesn't call. He doesn't text."

Chirpy gasped. "You don't think . . ."

"Think what?"

"That he's cheating," Chirpy continued. "I mean, those are the classic signs. I read about it in a magazine."

"Santiago would never do that," Lily-Rose said, folding her arms across her chest. "He's a good guy. He and Bex have been friends since forever."

That was all true. But what if there was another girl? What if he had met someone else and decided that he didn't want to go out with me anymore, but he just didn't know how to tell me? I would be devastated, not to mention humiliated. Once a person got dumped and replaced, it spread like wildfire through Lincoln Middle. I couldn't imagine how hard it would be to live down.

"You're right, I guess," Chirpy admitted. "Santiago wouldn't do that."

I sat on my bed with my mind reeling. For the first time in my life, I had a boyfriend whom I liked who actually liked me back. He didn't care that I wasn't super-girly. Santiago actually loved my tomboy ways. We had fun together. I thought everything was going great. Sometimes I thought we would actually outlive the shelf life of the normal middle-school relationship, which seemed to be three months at the most. The only couple who had surpassed that was MavRose—Maverick and Lily-Rose. They had been dating for almost three years and couldn't have been happier. I'd hoped that Santiago and I could have something like that.

Just then, everyone screamed. Standing in my doorway was my classmate and next door neighbor Sherry Silverstein, whom everyone at school referred to as Scary Sherry.

"Hey, Sherry," I said, trying to sound as cheerful as possible even though I was down in the dumps.

Sherry had definitely earned her nickname. Her skin was sickly pale and she had long jet-black hair that hung in her face that she never bothered to tuck behind her ear. She always wore all black and had the tendency to sneak up on people. Seriously, you wouldn't even hear her coming and she'd be right there scaring the living daylights out of you. Recently there was even a rumor going around that she was a vampire.

"Hey, Sherry," the girls muttered. They were still a little wary of her.

"Come on in," I told her and she took a seat at my desk.

I filled her in. "We were just talking about boys. Mainly Santiago."

"Oh, what a coincidence. I just ran into him at the mall," she replied.

Everyone gasped and looked at me. "The mall? What was he doing there?" I asked.

"I was shopping for a graduation dress with my mom, and I spotted him and a girl sitting in the food court drinking slushies. Blue slushies."

My friends gasped again, even louder this time.

I leapt from my bed. "Blue slushies? Blue slushies are our thing!" Every time we went to the mall, Santiago and I would ask the guys behind the counter at the slushie shop to mix the lemon and sour apple slushies together, forming the perfect flavor. How dare he share that with someone else? "Tell me about this girl."

"I'd never seen her before. She looked a couple of years older than us and she was very beautiful. Tan skin, long dark curly hair. Slender."

So not like me.

Chirpy shook her head. "The older woman. Boys fall for them every time."

Lily-Rose hopped up. "Let's go, girls. I'll flatten the tires on his bike. Chirpy and Marishca, you TP his yard. Bex, you get him in a headlock and then I'll kick the slushie out of him!"

Everyone stared at her for a moment before Chirpy urged her to sit back down. "Come back, Lily-Rose. Come back."

"What's going on?" Sherry asked.

"I think Santiago is cheating on me," I said quietly.

"Oh, Bex," Sherry said softly. "We've talked about this before. Don't go jumping to conclusions. There could be a perfectly fine explanation for this. She could just be a friend or something."

"But he lied to me, Sherry. He said he had to go straight home and help his mom do something, but then he turns up at the mall. We had plans."

"Oh," Sherry said. Even she had to admit there was something fishy about that.

Lily-Rose was still wound up. "Tell us about their body language, Sherry. Were they holding hands? Staring deeply into each other's eyes?"

"I only saw them briefly, but I didn't notice any of that. Bex, I'm sure it's nothing. Don't worry. Santiago's crazy about you. I sit next to him in science, and he's always scribbling your name over and over in his notebook instead of paying attention to Mr. Sayers."

"Really?" That made me feel a little better, but still . . .

When the girls left I found Aunt Jeanie in her bedroom putting some new clothes away in her humongous closet that was bigger than a lot of people's bedrooms.

"Aunt Jeanie, can I talk to you for a minute?"

"Of course. What's up?"

"What would you do if the person you were in a relationship with was cheating on you?"

Aunt Jeanie dropped the dress she was holding. "What? What do you know, Bex? Who is she? I'll kill Bob!"

"No! This has nothing to do with Uncle Bob! Calm down."

She took a deep breath. "Oh, of course not. Well, if someone *was* being unfaithful to me, I would end the relationship. Simple as that. He's obviously someone I can't trust, and he's not being respectful of my feelings." Aunt

Jeanie eyed me suspiciously. "Who are we talking about, Bex?"

I didn't want to tell her the truth because technically I wasn't supposed to be going out with Santiago. Aunt Jeanie had said that I wasn't allowed to have a boyfriend until I was sixteen. Besides, as Sherry said, I didn't even know if he were cheating on me for sure.

"No one. I was just wondering."

I couldn't tell if Aunt Jeanie believed me or not because she watched me from the corner of her eye. "Okay."

I turned to leave.

"Bex?"

"Yes, Aunt Jeanie?"

"This isn't about you, is it?"

My throat tightened. Did she know? How could she know? "No, Aunt Jeanie. I can't date yet, remember?"

She paused for a moment and I thought she was about to bust me. Instead she walked over and stroked my hair. "That's right, but when you do start dating, remember, you are too beautiful and amazing to be with anyone who would treat you less than what you're worth, and you're priceless. Don't forget that."

"Okay, Aunt Jeanie."

It wasn't every day I got compliments like that from her, but I knew she was right. I deserved better. If Santiago was seeing someone else, we were so over.

Chapter 4

The Worst Weekend Ever!

#sotraumatized

The rest of the week at school was much of the same: Santiago acting weird, Jeeves stressed out about his Language Arts grade, Lily-Rose wanting to jump Santiago, and Ava G. acting sour about not getting her way with the Graduation Committee. All that was so much more than what any eighth-grader should deal with, but Aunt Jeanie didn't see it that way. It was like she woke up that morning and asked herself, "How can I make my niece completely miserable?" Honestly, sometimes I asked myself what I ever did to deserve some of the things she did to me.

She pretty much tackled me the moment I walked into the door after school on that Friday afternoon. "Bex, I have the best news for you!"

I knew my aunt well enough not to get excited. Her good news was usually my tragedy. "What is it, Aunt Jeanie?" I asked wearily.

She sat on the sofa and patted the area next to her. "Have a seat."

I sat down and took a deep breath, bracing myself.

"You need to go upstairs right now and start packing because you and I are going to be spending the weekend at the Golden Springs Resort and Spa with the Groves."

Like I said, her good news was my tragedy. I blinked a few times trying to process the information. "Um . . . that sounds really nice and everything, but I can't. See, I'm going to the skating rink later with Santiago—and all my other friends," I added quickly so she wouldn't think it was a date.

"Bex, you can go to the skating rink with your friends any old time. This will be a great opportunity for you and Ava to spend some quality time together and bond."

I scowled at her. "Why is it so important to you guys that Ava and I become friends? What does it matter?"

"Well, Mrs. Groves and I are best friends and it would be so much nicer for us if you girls could get along, considering all the time we spend together. Besides, Ava is going places and the Groves have excellent connections.

They are just the type of people you want to be in with. I keep telling you, it's all about who you know."

I should have known. "Okay, that is like the dumbest reason ever to become friends with someone."

"Bex!" Aunt Jeanie yelled sharply. "This is not up for debate. Go upstairs and pack a bag. There's a car coming to pick us up at seven o'clock sharp."

She patted my knee and raced off to the kitchen to boss the housekeeper around. I huffed up to my room and accepted my fate. Think about Australia, Bex. Think about Australia.

The first thing I had to do was call Santiago and let him know our date for the skating rink that night was off. He answered his phone on the seventh ring.

"Hey, Bex," he said, sounding cheerful, but a phony cheerful.

"Hey, Santiago. Listen, I have bad news. Aunt Jeanie is making me go on this stupid weekend trip with the Groves so I'm going to have to cancel tonight."

There was a brief pause on his end. "Cancel what?"

"Cancel what? Santiago, we're supposed to be going to the skating rink tonight, remember? What's up with you lately?"

"Oh . . . oh, yeah. Sorry, that completely skipped my mind. Okay, it's cool if you have to cancel. I totally understand."

I hated that he didn't sound the least bit disappointed. He sounded relieved even. "I bet it is. What's going on with you?" I could hear a girl's voice in the background. Santiago didn't have a sister, and that definitely wasn't his mother. "Santiago, who is that?"

"Uh, who's who? No one. Listen, Bex, I have to go. Have fun on your trip. Call me when you get there. I'm sorry. I have to go." Then the line went dead. He was sorry about what?

I wanted to call my friends and let them know what was going on. I needed their advice, but Aunt Jeanie called me downstairs where she was already standing next to her packed designer luggage. I counted four bags.

"Aunt Jeanie, we're only going for the weekend, right?" She looked like she had enough for a month.

"Yes, Bex," she answered, not catching my drift. "How is your packing coming along? I will be up shortly to inspect."

Just then, I spotted my aunt's terrible triplets, Penelope, Priscilla, and Francois upstairs hanging over the banister. "Mommy, are you going somewhere?" Francois asked.

"Yes, dear," Aunt Jeanie called sweetly.

"For how long?" he demanded. Francois was a total momma's boy and acted like he would die if he went one day without Aunt Jeanie.

"Just for the weekend, pumpkin."

"Can't we come?" Penelope whined.

"No, sweetheart. Just Bex and I are going."

Priscilla gasped. "Bex is going to be gone for the whole weekend! Yes!"

Then the three of them danced around and cheered as if *I* were the annoying one. As usual, Aunt Jeanie ignored their poor behavior. She pushed me toward the stairs. "Make sure you pack a couple of swim suits."

I groaned. After shoving my way through the dancing triplets at the top of the stairs, I marched to my room and threw a bunch of random things in a bag. I didn't care what I took or what I looked like. I just wanted to press a button and fast forward to Sunday night when this dreadful trip would be over.

At seven on the dot, Aunt Jeanie was screaming at me to get my butt down the stairs. My eight-year-old sister Reagan was waiting by the door, looking a little sad. "I'm going to miss you, Bex," she whined, wrapping her arms around my waist. *At least somebody would*, I thought, throwing dirty looks at the triplets as they hugged Aunt Jeanie.

"I'm going to miss you too, Ray. Be good for Nana and Uncle Bob." Our grandmother was coming to help out for the weekend.

"Okay," she said unconvincingly as she skipped away. I loved my little sister, but she could be a handful. I did, however, feel guilty about leaving her alone with the triplets. The four of them got along like cats and water.

The driver placed our bags in the back of the car and opened the doors for us to climb inside. Ava and Mrs. Groves were already in the car. Aunt Jeanie and Mrs. Groves exchanged air kisses while Ava and I rolled our eyes at each other. She had headphones over her ears and I planned to put mine on. I was not going to spend this trip trying to make forced conversation with her.

"So," Mrs. Groves said as the car pulled off. "The drive is about an hour and a half. We can have a late dinner when we get there, change into our pajamas, and then have some girl talk. It'll be like a good old slumber party."

"Yay," I said unenthusiastically. Ava cracked the gum she was chewing and said nothing.

Aunt Jeanie and Mrs. Groves became engrossed in their own conversation about gossip and nonsense and I turned on my music to tune everyone out. I had just dozed off when we arrived at the resort.

The Golden Springs Resort was an upscale, expensive place. Aunt Jeanie went often, but I had never been. The resort had restaurants, a spa, amazing pools, a game room, a night club and lots of other things. I decided to look on the bright side and make the most out of this trip.

We made our way into the lobby as the driver and bellhops unloaded our luggage and bought it in. Mrs. Groves went to the front desk to check in and grab our hotel keys. A moment later, she came back.

"Here you are girls," she said handing Ava and me each something that looked like a credit card. "Your room key. We'll be right across the hall from you."

"Excuse me?" Ava asked. "We're not rooming together?" she asked, glaring at her mother.

Mrs. Groves pinched her daughter's cheek. "No, we thought it would be best if you two roomed together alone. It'll help you get to know each other better."

I already knew everything I needed to know about Ava. I looked to Aunt Jeanie, hoping she would tell me Mrs.

Groves was joking, but she only nodded. "Let's go," she said as she led us toward the elevator.

"Wait," I said. "You're just going to let two fourteen-year-olds stay in a hotel room unsupervised? I have to say, that's very irresponsible of you, Aunt Jeanie. I'm shocked."

Aunt Jeanie smiled at me. "Oh, Bex, we'll be right across the hall and we'll definitely be checking in on you from time to time. We trust you girls."

Of course, she would have to pick that very moment to decide to be cool. If I had wanted to stay in the hotel room with one of my friends, she would have had a heart attack.

The rest of us moved toward the elevator, but Ava stood planted in the same spot as if she couldn't believe what was happening. I hoped she knew that I was just as disgusted by our rooming arrangements as she was.

In our rooms, we unpacked silently and then went down to one of the resort's restaurants for dinner. I ordered chicken fingers and fries, which is usually one of my favorite meals, but that night it tasted like cardboard. Knowing I would have to spend the weekend with Ava had left a nasty taste in my mouth. The two of us chewed our meals silently as we listened to Aunt Jeanie and Mrs. Groves gab about a huge upcoming party one of their friends was throwing. They seemed to be enjoying themselves, not caring at all that Ava and I looked completely miserable.

Back in the room, Ava and I maneuvered around each other, not speaking or making eye contact. It wasn't an easy thing to do. She managed to weasel her way into the shower first even though she saw I was about to go in, but I didn't object. It wasn't worth fighting over.

After we showered and climbed into bed, Ava ordered a movie without even asking me if I wanted to see it also. Of course, I found that to be rude and inconsiderate, but this was Ava we were talking about. I hated chick flicks and I was pretty sure the movie she'd chosen fit into that category.

"Aren't you even going to ask what I want to see?"

"No," she said curtly. "If you don't want to watch it, go to sleep."

I made a face at her and rolled over in my bed. It turned out the movie was actually a good action flick that I wanted to see, but I wasn't about to give her the satisfaction of my watching it. Somewhere in the middle, with the covers pulled over my head, amid the noise of car crashes and gunshots, I drifted off to sleep. My last thoughts were of Santiago—what was he doing and with whom?

The next morning Ava was still asleep when I got up to get dressed. Aunt Jeanie had texted me earlier that morning:

Mrs. Groves and I are going to spend the day shopping and going to the spa. You girls have fun at the resort. Order room service for breakfast. There are so many things for you to do together! Have fun. Will check in later.

Yeah, right. They hadn't checked in on us once. They were obviously more concerned with enjoying their own weekend.

I groaned and promptly decided that I would be spending the day at the pool by myself. It's not like the adults were there to make sure we hung out together. I took my time getting dressed and brushing my hair. When I exited the bathroom, Ava was perched on her bed giving me her stink-eye, which seemed meaner than usual.

"What's your problem?" I asked, rubbing sunblock onto my arms. I hadn't even spoken to her yet. What could I have possibly done? Then I remembered that just my mere existence irked Ava.

"What gives you the right?"

"What are you talking about?"

She flung something on my bed. "What gives you the right to write such horrible things about me?"

My heart sunk once I realized the object she had flung over to my bed was my journal. Admittedly, I had written some pretty horrible things about Ava in there, but she deserved every single word of it.

"What is wrong with you?" I screamed. "You don't read another girl's journal! That's . . . that's just deplorable . . . disgusting . . . and illegal!"

Ava scrunched her face up at me. "It's not illegal, stupid. I demand that you erase every single thing you've written about me in there right now or I'll sue you for libel."

"Oh, now who's stupid?" I asked. "You can't sue someone for what she writes in her personal diary. It wasn't for your beady little eyes anyway." I grabbed my journal from the bed and shoved it to the bottom of my suitcase. "Don't touch it again!"

I took the phone and dialed 000.

"What are you doing?" Ava asked as the phone rang.

"Not that it's any of your business, but I'm ordering breakfast."

"Oh, order breakfast for me too," she said as if she hadn't just broken one of the cardinal rules of girlhood: Thou shalt never read another girl's journal. "I want—"

"I don't care what you want!" I screamed, just as someone picked up on the other end.

"Hello," she said, sounding a bit confused. "Golden Springs Room Service."

"Yes," I said. "I'd like an order of French toast and a side of bacon. Also a glass of orange juice."

"I want a fruit salad," Ava said in the background, but I waved her away.

"NO FRUIT SALAD!" I shouted into the phone.

"Okay," said the lady on the other end. "French toast, bacon, orange juice, and no fruit salad. Will that be all for you this morning?"

"Yes, that'll be all," I said loudly, looking at Ava. The lady probably thought I was crazy.

"Okay, it'll be right up," she said.

"Thanks." I hung up, but I kept my hand on the phone.

"You are such a brat!" Ava spat as she tried to grab the phone from me.

I held the phone even tighter. "Excuse me, I have to make a call."

"You do not. Let go, so I can order my breakfast."

I know. I know. There are lots of times when I could take the high road to avoid getting into it with Ava, but I just couldn't stand how she always got her way. And I wasn't too keen on taking orders from her. Besides, I was still angry about my journal and all the other things she had done to me.

I was much stronger than her and I was not letting go of that phone. Ava jumped on my back and we fell to the ground wrestling. If only Mrs. Groves and Aunt Jeanie could have seen us. It would serve them right for leaving us alone.

"Give . . . me . . . the . . . phone," Ava said, sounding winded.

"Never," I said, feeling perfectly fine. I could have gone on that way forever.

Finally, she gave up, grabbed her cell phone and headed for the bathroom. "I hate you with a passion!" she shouted. "A great, burning passion!"

"The feeling is mutual!" I shouted as she slammed the bathroom door.

Moments later, we ate our breakfasts in stony silence, and I left to go down to the pool. I stayed there as long as I could without the risk of being sunburned and then spent the rest of the time in the game room challenging a nine-year-old at pinball.

I could have stayed in the game room all day, but the kid's mom showed up and said they had somewhere to go.

Hoping that Ava was still out, I made my way back up to our room.

Aunt Jeanie and Mrs. Groves finally showed up a little after six in the evening. They knocked on our door and I let them in. "Where have you two been?"

They pranced past me, laughing and looking extremely happy. At least someone was having fun. "Oh," Mrs. Groves said, "we found the best shopping mall down the street. Maybe we can take you girls tomorrow. I know Ava would love it."

"No, thanks," I said as I plopped down on the bed.

"Where is Ava?" her mother asked.

I shrugged. "Siberia, hopefully."

"Bex Carter!" Aunt Jeanie snapped. "Really, where is she? You guys are supposed to be hanging out together."

"That's not really working out too well. By the way," I said to Mrs. Groves, "can you please tell you daughter it is extremely rude and unacceptable to read another person's journal. That's just common courtesy."

Aunt Jeanie smiled sweetly at Mrs. Groves. "Please excuse us for a second," Aunt Jeanie said, grabbing my arm and dragging me into the bathroom.

I wasn't usually afraid of Aunt Jeanie, but I was at that moment. She pointed her finger in my face and spoke in a low voice. That's how I knew when Aunt Jeanie was really mad—she didn't yell, she whispered.

"You will behave yourself and stop being incessantly rude or I will cancel that trip to Australia so fast and ship you off to a boarding school for all your high school years. Control that mouth of yours. Got it?"

I gulped. Yep, I definitely had it. "Yes, Aunt Jeanie."

Then she smiled at me, which turned out to be extremely creepy. "Good," she said, before opening the bathroom door and walking out.

(Shivers.)

"The point," Mrs. Groves said, "was for the two of you to bond. How is that going to happen when you're not together?"

I didn't know, and I didn't care, but I did want to go to Australia. Mrs. Groves called Ava's phone and discovered that she was getting a manicure. "You know what I think?" Mrs. Groves said. "We had planned on taking you girls to a show tonight, but I think tonight the two of you should just hang out here. Have dinner together and talk. I think that would help a lot." Apparently, she thought locking us in our room and forcing us to get along would work.

Ava got back and acted mortified about the idea, but neither of us had any choice. In our room, we ate our dinners in silence and then sat on our beds watching television.

"I'm sorry. I didn't know you really liked him," Ava said out of the blue.

"What?" I asked, not taking my eyes off the television.

"Harold. I'm sorry about that. I honestly didn't know you liked him."

Harold Kline was a sore spot for me and one of the many reasons I couldn't stand Ava. A while ago, Ava and I were helping Harold run for president. Ava decided that having a girlfriend would be good for his image and I ended up being that girlfriend. Surprisingly, Harold and I actually fell for each other and I thought at the time that he was a great guy. After he won the election, Ava decided that dating Ava T. would be better for Harold's popularity so he started going out with her just like that. I was crushed. Setting Harold up with Ava T. was all Ava's idea and their relationship ended up lasting only a couple of weeks.

Harold has seen the error of his ways since then and has professed his undying love for me numerous times, but I had moved on. Still, Harold had been my first real heartbreak.

"I don't want to talk about Harold," I said bitterly.

"Okay, but you have to understand that I honestly didn't know. I thought you were going out with him just as a favor to help him win the election and once the election was over, I thought you guys were too. I had no idea until I read your journal . . . I'm sorry about that too."

I glanced over at her and she really did look sorry. I'd never seen her look that way before and it was kind of strange. I wondered what was bringing on this sudden change of heart. "I can't believe you're actually apologizing for something."

"Heartbreak is the worst feeling in the world, and I don't want to be the one responsible for any girl getting her heart broken . . . even if it's you."

Now that was more like it.

She looked away from me and down at her newly polished toes. "I mean it, Bex. It happened to me not too long ago."

Ava looked as if she were about to cry. I totally didn't want that, but I was curious. Ava was known as the heartbreaker. All the boys liked her, and I couldn't imagine anyone breaking her heart. "What happened?"

She paused as if debating whether or not she should tell me.

"I was going out with this guy, a tenth-grader. I met him at our country club. It made me feel so special to be dating a kid in high school. I thought Grayson really liked me. Well, I learned from one of my friends who goes to Lincoln High that I was just Grayson's country club girlfriend and that he had a real girlfriend at school. When she heard about me, she demanded that Grayson dump me and he did . . . on my birthday! At my own party!"

Wow, that was pretty bad. "I'm sorry, Ava. Really."

She nodded. "Getting your heart broken feels like . . . like . . ."

"Someone ripped out your heart, stomped on it, and then ran it through the blender?" I offered.

She smiled a little. "Yeah, just like that."

We were quiet for a few moments.

"But," Ava said, "if I hadn't broken you and Harold up, you wouldn't be dating Santiago, and that's going really well, isn't it?"

I lay back on my bed. "Uh, yeah. It's great."

She gave me the side-eye. "You're lying. What's up?"

There was a lot I needed to get off my chest. I wanted to talk about Santiago, I wanted to confide in Ava, but even though she was being nice in that moment, I didn't trust her. Ava was very good at acting, and she could have very well been playing me just to get information. I didn't need her telling the other Avas that I thought Santiago had another girlfriend and throwing it in my face.

"Nothing," I replied.

She sighed and stared at the television. I was still a little taken aback by her apology. I knew the two of us would never really be friends, but we could at least be civil to one another and if we could do that, we could trick my aunt and her mother into thinking that we were really friends.

"Ava, I really, really want to go on that trip to Australia with my Aunt Alice and I know you really want to go to that dance camp, and at this rate we're both going to be spending our summer on a farm with your grandparents."

Ava made a gagging sound.

"So, I propose we make a pact."

She narrowed her eyes at me. "What kind of pact?"

"That we pretend to be friends at least when the grown-ups are around. At school we can go on hating each other as usual, but in front of them we'll be BFFs."

Ava thought about it for a minute. "I really want to go to Camp Pointe more than anything." She shrugged. "Okay. Sounds good to me."

And that is how Ava Groves became my BFF—Bogus Fake Friend.

Chapter 5

Totes Adorbs

—feeling grossed out ☹

The next day I was awakened by Ava speaking loudly on the phone, undoubtedly to the other Avas. I was determined to be patient with her so that we could make nice in front of Aunt Jeanie and Mrs. Groves, but the fact that she was speaking ten times louder than she needed to early in the morning was making it extremely difficult.

"Yeah, so I'm wearing my new swimsuit today and it's totes adorbs . . . yeah . . . it's hot pink and one of the straps has little rosettes on it . . . I have flip-flops to match that are also totes adorbs."

Somebody, please put me out of my misery.

"Hold on, Ava," Ava said when she looked over and saw me awake. "The four of us are spending the day at the pool."

I rolled my eyes. That was the last thing I wanted to do. On top of pretending to be BFFs with Ava, I was going to have to subject myself to being body-shamed by three people who were no larger than the "perfect" size.

We ate breakfast, and I changed into my swimsuit. It was my first time wearing a two-piece, and I actually kind of liked it. Aunt Jeanie called it a tankini. She had made it very clear that I would not be allowed to wear a bikini until I was thirty. That was fine with me.

The suit was teal with yellow polka dots. Looking at myself in the mirror, I felt a little self-conscious. Aunt Jeanie always told me how I was "well-endowed" for my age. My friends were envious of my chest, but I wasn't ecstatic about it. I didn't like the attention it brought to me especially when I was wearing a swimsuit. Usually when I swam, I preferred to wear a T-shirt and a pair of shorts, but Aunt Jeanie had forbidden that. She said that proper young ladies wore proper bathing suits. It was easy for her to say when her body looked awesome in anything.

I reached for my cover-up when I realized I had forgotten to bring it into the bathroom with me. I could think of nothing worse than strutting out of the bathroom in my bathing suit in front of Ava, who was probably sitting on the bed looking "totes adorbs" while applying sunscreen.

I grabbed my towel from the rack and wrapped it around myself before leaving the bathroom. Just as I suspected, Ava sat on the bed waiting and watching.

This was going to require some smooth operating. Somehow I was going to have to remove my towel and put on my cover-up while not exposing my bathing suit. Apparently, I wasn't very good at that because as soon as I reached for my cover-up, the towel dropped to the ground.

Ava gasped, and I braced myself for a vicious comment. "Bex, that suit is totes adorbs."

After I recovered from the shock of her compliment, I managed to say, "Uh, thanks, Ava. Aunt Jeanie picked it out."

"She has good taste. Don't put that on, you're covering it up," she said as I slid into my cover-up. Did she really mean that or was she trying to set me up to go out in public and embarrass myself?

"I know but, I like to cover . . . you know."

"Your boobs?"

I nodded. Ava shrugged and reached for her tote bag, tossing a magazine inside. "I don't know why. Everyone is jealous of them."

"They are?" I asked, slightly happy and slightly horrified that people were talking about my boobs. I knew my friends did, but *everyone*?

"Yeah." Ava looked me up and down. "You've slimmed down some."

"What's that supposed to mean?" I demanded.

"Just what I said, that you've slimmed down some. What's your problem?"

"My problem is you, calling me fat!" I slipped into my cover-up convinced that she was in fact trying to set me up.

Ava jumped up from the bed with her bag on her shoulder just as there was a knock on the door. "I didn't call you fat. I simply stated that you're smaller than you used to be. That's all. I thought we were being friends today," she said as she headed to open the door.

She was right. I was so used to her insulting my looks, I guess I had jumped the gun. Aunt Jeanie and Mrs. Groves were waiting for us. I had to admit they looked great. They both had on bikini tops and sarongs wrapped around their waists. Not bad for moms.

"You guys look totes adorbs," Ava told them, and I had to close my eyes and count to ten. It was going to be a long day.

At the pool, the issue of removing my cover-up became a non-issue when Aunt Jeanie demanded that I leave it on. Mrs. Groves had suggested I take it off to show off my cute bathing suit, but when I did, Aunt Jeanie's eyes practically bulged out of her head, making me feel super embarrassed.

"Bex, put those things away," she snapped staring at my chest. "Put it back on right now," she said, tossing me the cover-up and looking down at her own boobs, which were actually smaller than mine.

I really wanted to go in the water, but since Ava and I were pretending to bond, I sat in the lounge chair next to hers where she sat reading a magazine.

"Want to get in?" I asked.

"No way. This bathing suit isn't made for swimming. It's just for looking cute."

I looked around. The pool area was full of families and people having a good time. No one was paying her any attention. "Looking cute for whom?"

Ava sighed as if I had asked the dumbest question in the world. "The masses, Bex. You never know who's around to take a picture of you and post it on social media. A girl must look flawless at all times."

This was surely advice she had learned from the ever-insightful Chanel Featherstone.

Ava leaned over. "Here. Look at this magazine with me. Let's laugh like we're reading something really funny."

I did as she said even though I felt incredibly stupid. After a few minutes I stopped. The heat was sweltering and I couldn't take it anymore. "I'm going for a dip," I told her. I dove into the deep end of the pool, cover-up and all, even though I wanted to take it off. No one else was swimming in a cover-up, but I didn't need Aunt Jeanie freaking out on me.

I swam for a bit until Aunt Jeanie said we needed to get ready for dinner. The rest of the weekend went by like a blur. It definitely wasn't as bad as I had expected it to be. I mean, Ava and I had actually roomed together without killing each other and we'd figured out a way to save our summers. The only bad thing about the weekend besides hearing Ava say "totes adorbs" repeatedly was that Santiago hadn't called or texted me once.

Chapter 6
Do I Have To Go?

—feeling anxious ☹

Journal #19

I'm doing something that I feel pretty guilty about—being fake, even though it is for a good reason. I hate having to pretend that I'm friends with Ava, but it's the only way I can save myself from shoveling cow poop all summer and spending each and every day with Ava on some boring farm. She was actually pretty decent to me for a few minutes on our weekend trip. Maybe, just maybe, we can actually pull this off.

With all the stuff going on with Ava and Santiago, I had to admit that I hadn't given much thought to high school, and I definitely wasn't as excited as some of the other kids.

After Maverick had told this hilarious joke at the lunch table, Jeeves made an unsettling observation. "This might be the last few weeks that we'll all have lunch together."

"Yeah, that's true," Chirpy said. "Lincoln High has two lunch shifts so we might not even have the same lunch time."

What? Why was I just hearing about this? What if all my friends had a different lunch time and I had to eat lunch all by myself?

Lily-Rose and Marishca looked at each other. Marishca jabbed Lily-Rose in the ribs with her elbow. I could tell when my best friends were hiding something.

"What is it?" I asked wearily.

"Well, you know Marishca and I got accepted into the performing arts program at Lincoln High," Lily-Rose said.

"Yes," I said slowly because I knew something bad was about to follow.

"Well," Lily-Rose continued. "It seems that all the performing arts students take their classes together so—"

"You won't have any classes with us?" Chirpy shouted. Several kids looked at us to see what was going on.

"No," Marishca said quietly.

"That's awful," I said. "I may never see you guys. Not even after school." The performing arts students got dismissed an hour and a half after everyone else because they took extra classes.

"Sorry," Lily-Rose said, looking down at the table as if she had done something wrong.

"It's not your fault," I told her. "It's just that everything is going to change and I don't like it."

"Life is all about change, Bex," Chirpy said, sounding like my Nana.

"I know, Chirpy, I know," I said, groaning. Just then, Ava came and leaned over our table. Everyone glared at her, wondering what evil she was up to. She only stopped by our table to insult someone.

"Can we help you?" Santiago asked. Once again he had been quiet most of the time.

"No," Ava snapped. "I need to speak to Bex, not you."

"What is it?" I asked.

Ava said the next words slowly and deliberately as if it pained her. "Will you eat lunch at my table?"

My friends all gasped as if a spaceship had just landed outside or something.

"Why? We don't have to put on a show here."

Ava leaned in closer. "I think we do. I'm pretty sure my mother has spies here." I looked around and sighed. Lots of kids had their eyes on us, probably wondering why Ava was hovering above my lowly table. I wouldn't put it past

Mrs. Groves to hunt down her friends who had kids who went to Lincoln Middle to ask them to spy on us.

"Why can't you sit here?" I asked. I had no desire to be around the other Avas and their lackeys when I didn't have to. One Ava was bad enough. Also, the boys they hung out with were total jerks.

My friends, of course, knew about the arrangement Ava and I had made while at Golden Springs, but they looked affronted that I had asked her to sit with us. I guessed it wasn't really fair to punish them for something that was between Ava and me.

Chirpy shook her head vigorously. "Don't do it, Bex. A million trips to the moon aren't worth spending one minute at the Wicked Witch Table."

Ava scrunched her face up at her. "Shut up, Twerpy! Bex, are you coming or not?" I glanced around the cafeteria. Any one of those kids could have been a spy who was watching us to see how we interacted with one another.

Santiago was staring down at his pizza, oblivious to what was going on. I doubted he would mind whether or not I went.

"Fine," I said, grabbing my things. "I'll see you guys later for our committee meeting."

I dragged myself across the cafeteria to Ava's table, which was full of kids I didn't like and would never hang out with.

Ava G. tapped Ava M. on the shoulder. "Over."

Obediently Ava M. slid over, making room for me to sit next to Ava G. The table became quiet and everyone stared at me as if I were some type of creature they had never seen before. Since no one was speaking, I assumed Ava had told them what was going on. I silently took a bite of my grilled cheese sandwich. Maybe if I kept my head down and my mouth full of food, I could survive the remainder of the lunch period.

Ava G. cleared her throat. "So, Bex, I was just telling everyone here about our time in Golden Springs." Of course she was. Ava G. loved nothing more than to brag about her fabulous life. "Room service, massages, manis, pedis, it was wonderful." The girls at the table looked impressed and even a little envious.

"Yeah," I said. That was about all I could think to add to the conversation.

Ava M. turned to me. "Bex, now that you and Ava are '*friends*' (she had put air quotes around the word friends), I hope you'll be on our side in the rest of our graduation committee meetings. Everything was going so well until you joined and now it's all turning into a tacky mess."

Nope. I was wrong. I wasn't going to make it. "Everything was going well in your eyes because all the other kids were doing exactly what you wanted them to do and not voicing their opinions and just because Ava and I are 'best buds' (I put "best buds" in air quotes) now, doesn't mean that I have to go along with everything she says."

Ava G. sighed on the other side of me. I felt as if I were in the middle of an annoyed mean girl sandwich.

"Honestly, Bex, why do you have to make this harder than it has to be? I just need you to agree with me on one little thing, the class song."

I knew this was going to be the biggest issue because everyone had such different tastes, but I thought most of us were going to be able to come to a consensus on one particular song. "What song were you thinking of?" I asked, knowing that she was about to say something ridiculous.

"'Platinum Girl' by the Pink Boas."

I should have known. "Platinum Girl" was an entire song dedicated to how perfect and beautiful the girl group thought they were and how hideous and jealous the rest of us were.

"That is the dumbest idea I've ever heard. What does being conceited and thinking you're all that have to do with graduating? That song is totally shallow. We need something we can all relate to."

"Yeah," said a boy named Chad. "I'm not singing 'Platinum Girl.' No way."

"Shush, Chad!" Ava snapped. "We need something hip and cool, and that's the number one song on the charts right now, Bex. Back me up on this," she ordered.

I stood as the bell rang. I knew we had to be pretending to get along, but I was drawing the line there. I was going to have to disagree with Ava in the committee meeting whether she liked it or not.

The beginning of the meeting was full of kids playing music on their phones trying to decide which song they liked best. I took it upon myself to write the top three choices on the board so that we could take a final count.

Just before the vote, Ava's hand shot up. "I'd like to request that 'Platinum Girl' be added to the ballot, please."

No one wanted that song except for her and the other Avas, but I wrote it on the board just to humor her. "Okay, let's vote," I said. "All in favor of 'Just One More Night' by the Buey Boys, raise your hand." I counted. "Okay, eight votes," I said writing the number on the board. " 'Always There' by Miranda Lilac. Three votes. 'Friends Forever' by George Culliver.' " Ten hands shot up. The last song was Ava's lame suggestion. I could tell by the number of votes already on the board that her selection wasn't going to get many votes. I think Ava could sense that too because she already had this sour expression on her face. I cleared my throat trying not to laugh. "All in favor of 'Platinum Girl' by the Pink Boas, raise your hands." The only hands that went up belonged to people named Ava. "'Friends Forever' it is," I announced and everyone cheered.

Chirpy hopped up. "That was the only thing on our agenda today, so meeting adjourned. We'll meet again on Wednesday."

Ava G. shot Chirpy a nasty look for taking charge, but Chirpy either didn't notice or didn't care.

Everyone filed out of the room as I searched for an eraser to clean Mrs. Diaz's board. Just as I spotted one, someone said, "Thanks a lot, Bex," from behind me. I jumped because I thought everyone had left the room.

"Really, Ava. It wasn't my fault. Everyone had a vote."

She wasn't satisfied with that answer. "Yeah, because you didn't have my back. If you would have acted like you liked the song, they would have liked it too. You see how they listen to you."

"I wasn't about to pretend to like that god-awful song, whether we're friends or not."

Ava stormed to the front of the room and stopped in front of me as if she were going to hit me. I folded my arms across my chest to show her that I wasn't intimidated. "The committee has spoken. What are you going to do about it?"

She growled at me and did something incredibly stupid. She shoved me into Mrs. Diaz's desk. I expected a lot of things from Ava, but I hadn't expected her to do that. Her push was actually a lot harder than I'd ever imagined she could push.

I wanted to pummel her, but I thought about being on a plane on the way to Australia with my favorite aunt. Instead of punching her, I took the eraser and finished wiping the board. Apparently Ava hadn't had enough because when my back was turned, she hit me in the back with a highlighter from the teacher's desk.

That was it. I tackled Ava to the ground and once again we wrestled. I had Ava in a good headlock when we rolled into Mrs. Diaz's podium, knocking down a bunch of books and sheets of paper. The door to Mrs. Diaz's office swung open.

"Girls! Girls!" she shouted, getting on the floor and separating us. "What on earth is going on?"

Ava and I looked at each other and probably had the same terrifying thoughts. Mrs. Diaz was going to call our parents and tell them we had been fighting. That phone call would get us a one-way ticket to the farm for sure.

"Uh, Mrs. Diaz, we were just playing around," Ava said quickly. "Bex was talking about trying out for the girls' wrestling team next year at Lincoln High, and I was giving her some pointers."

Good save, Ava. Good save.

Mrs. Diaz looked at me with an eyebrow raised. I nodded.

I couldn't tell if she fully believed us, but she let it go. "Fine, but you guys know better than to be roughhousing in here. Clean up this mess," she said, looking at the array of books and papers on the floor.

Ava and I had begun to straighten up, thankful that we hadn't gotten into any real trouble, when I received a text.

It was Santiago telling me he wouldn't be able to come over that night to study for our math test as we had planned. Ava watched me as I glared at the message on my phone. "What?"

I frowned at her. "What do you care?"

She made a face at me. "I *don't* care," she said as she went back to shuffling papers.

I sighed. I was bursting with emotion and I needed to vent to someone. It took me a minute to decide between Ava and Mrs. Diaz's podium. I figured although I didn't like her, she knew a lot about boys. "It's Santiago. He's been acting weird lately. I think he's cheating on me."

Ava gasped. "Not Santiago. For some reason that goober's head-over-heels for you. I can tell."

I told her about all the missed dates and phone calls.

She thought for a moment. "You know, I missed all the clues with Grayson, but when Ava T. was dealing with this issue about a month ago, I was ready. She thought her BF was two-timing her and he was. Of course, I was the one who busted the creep."

"How'd you do it? I can't just walk up to him and ask him if he's cheating. Of course he's not going to own up to it."

Ava pulled her phone from her purse. "Leave it to me. If he's cheating, I'll find out. I can even tell you who and why. I'm on it."

I raised my eyebrows. "Why are you helping me? I just kicked your butt."

She looked up from her phone. "You did *not* just kick my butt, and we girls have to stick together in situations like this. Boys can't get away with treating us like dishrags."

I was trying to comprehend the fact that Ava was actually helping me while thinking I really didn't want to hear what she might find out. If Santiago was a two-timer, I . . . I . . . well, I wasn't sure how I would feel. Probably angry and betrayed.

Once we had Mrs. Diaz's room straightened up the way it was supposed to be, Ava and I gathered our things to leave.

"I've gathered my intel," Ava said. "I'll give you a report in the morning."

"How?" I asked. "You're going to follow Santiago around?"

"Me, follow that dweeb? No!"

I gave her a look.

"I, I mean, he's pretty cute—for Santiago—and he does make a lot of money so he can buy you things. He's nice. You could do worse. But no, I'm not going to be following him. I have eyes and ears everywhere, one of the advantages to being the most popular girl in school."

I wasn't so sure about her eyes and ears. "Whatever you say, Ava. Whatever you say."

"Maybe Jeeves has the right idea," I told Lily-Rose as we talked on the phone that night. I had already given her the rundown on Santiago and Ava, and she thought I was stupid to trust Ava. "Maybe we should all fail a class and stay in middle school another year, just to make sure we're ready."

"First of all, I don't think Jeeves is failing English on purpose. He seems pretty miserable about it, and second of all, why would we do that? I, for one, can't wait to go to high school. It's going to be a blast, I know it."

"Lily-Rose, how can you say that? We'll hardly see each other. I won't see you and Marishca at all. Maverick or Jeeves either. That school is going to be huge and with so many more kids, it's going to be hard for us to find each other. Then there's the lunch thing. What if we don't have the same lunch period? And high school guys, they're like full-grown men. They're not going to be anything like these immature boys in middle school."

"What do you care anyway? You're with Santiago."

I huffed. "Yeah, for now."

"Bex, relax. We're growing up. We're going to do different things and meet new friends and maybe not spend as much time together, but that doesn't mean that we're ever going to stop being friends. The Tribe is forever."

"Yeah, I guess," I said, but I wasn't really convinced. Something told me that after middle school my friendships with Lily-Rose, Chirpy, and Marishca wouldn't be the same. I couldn't imagine my life without those girls, and if going to high school was going to come between us, I would stay in middle school forever.

Chapter 7

Operation Make Jeeves Smarter

—feeling optimistic ☺

Journal Entry #20

I know this might seem corny, but I'm terrified of going to high school. Did you ever feel that way, Aunt Alice? I kind of like the way things are now (mostly) and I don't want them to change. Nobody else feels the way I do though. They can't wait for high school and that sort of makes me feel like there's something wrong with me.

Here are the cons of going to high school:

*a lot more kids

*more work/ harder classes

*new teachers to hate me for no reason

I won't see my friends so much. Lily-Rose, Marishca, Maverick, and Jeeves will all be in the Performing Arts Program.

high school boys – I'm just getting the hang of middle school boys. I'm so not ready for this.

There's probably a lot more things I can't think of at the moment.

There's nothing like starting the school day off by practically being tackled by Ava Groves. I was walking down the hallway minding my own business when someone grabbed me and pulled me into the girl's bathroom. Before I could say anything, Ava put her hand over my mouth. "Shh," she said, before locking the bathroom door.

The whole situation was a little creepy. Okay, it was a lot creepy. "What are you doing?" I demanded.

"I have my first report on that boyfriend of yours."

"Oh," I said, feeling a little light-headed. I prepared myself for the worst. "Lay it on me."

Ava pulled out her phone and began to read. "Well, from eight to three he was in school, of course, but after that it gets really interesting. On his way home from school he stopped by Alfred's Convenience Store and purchased *two* twenty-ounce bottles of soda. One grape and one orange."

She paused and waited for my reaction. When I said nothing she repeated, "*Two* sodas, Bex."

"I heard you," I replied impatiently. Normally, I would think, so what, he was really thirsty, but I knew for a fact that Santiago hated grape soda. That drink had been for somebody else. I shrugged. "He could have been buying a soda for anyone. What else?"

Ava rolled her eyes and looked back at her phone. "Okay . . . he got home around 3:20. At around four o'clock a van pulled up. Santiago ran out and got inside. My informant couldn't tell who was driving, but the van ended up at the movie theater, and Santiago and a very pretty girl got out and went inside."

My throat tightened. I had no reasonable explanation for that so I said nothing.

"Then," Ava continued, "after the movie the van picked them up and dropped the girl and Santiago off at Santiago's house where they stayed for a very, very long time. Then my informant had to go home and do his homework," Ava added quickly, putting her phone away.

"So what does all this mean?" I asked myself out loud, almost forgetting that Ava was there. My head was swirling with thoughts of Santiago's betrayal. How could he?

"I think you know, Bex. I'm real sorry."

The bell rang, and I was glad because I wanted the whole conversation to be over. More importantly, I didn't want Ava to see how hurt I was.

"We should go," I told her. "Thanks."

"No problem. Are you going to be okay?"

I forced a smile. "Of course. He's just a boy. It's no big deal." But I was lying. It was a huge, huge deal.

"Jeeves, who wrote the poem 'The Raven'?" I asked.

Jeeves looked at me and grimaced. "Uh, William Shakespeare?"

"William Shakespeare? *William Shakespeare*? Are you serious?" I could tell from his bewildered expression that he was.

The six of us were huddled in the library after school trying to help Jeeves brush up on his Language Arts so he could bring his grade up. He was having major trouble keeping up with Emily Dickinson, Edgar Allan Poe, and Robert Frost. I was sorely disappointed that Santiago was missing again because he was the best at this stuff and he had promised Jeeves that he would help him. Santiago could always come up with weird little ways to help you remember things. Not only was Santiago being a janky boyfriend, but he was being a bad friend.

Chirpy read him a sentence, a rather long one I'd have to say. "What is the preposition of the sentence?"

Jeeves frowned. "William Shakespeare?"

Oy vey.

We stayed for another hour until Mrs. Barnes, the librarian, kicked us out. Jeeves had answered William Shakespeare to almost every question he was asked. He was a smart kid, but I thought he was psyching himself out. He needed to relax and I was getting pretty worried for him. As we exited the school, Ava sent me a text.

"Coming 2 your house in 30 mins 2 pick u up. Something 2 show u."

My heart thudded. I knew this had something to do with Santiago, and if she had something to show me, it had to be bad. I didn't say anything to the others because I didn't want to talk about it. I hadn't even told them about Santiago's movie date with the mystery girl.

At home, I stood by the front door because Ava had texted me that she was on her way. "Bex, you're not going out," Aunt Jeanie said, passing by flipping through a catalog. "You just got here. Homework."

"But I'm going to the mall with Ava."

She paused and a huge smile spread across her face. "Oh, okay. Good to hear."

Of course. Going to the mall with Ava was much more important than homework.

A yellow mustang pulled up to the house, and Ava texted me that she was there. In the front seat was a boy who was clearly a high-schooler. Ava was in the front passenger seat wearing shades and texting. A boy who looked like a younger version of the boy driving sat in the back seat looking bored. I slid in next to him.

"Hey, everyone," I said as cheerfully as I could despite being confused. "I'm Bex."

"Bex, this is Chase," Ava said pointing to the boy sitting beside her. "He's Danny's older brother. Danny's my boyfriend."

I looked over and Danny gave me a weak smile. I didn't know him. He didn't go to our school, but he looked like a nice enough kid. I wondered why Ava wasn't sitting in the back next to him.

"Bex, if you end up breaking up with Santiago, make sure your next boyfriend has an older brother or sister with a car. It's so convenient."

Danny shook his head and stared out the window. It didn't take a rocket scientist to figure out that Ava was using this poor kid for his older brother's transportation. Reason 9,732,938 why I didn't like Ava. She was a liar and master manipulator.

I had felt sorry for her when she told me that story about Grayson, but maybe that was payback for the way she treated guys, which was mostly like dirt.

"You guys are going to love Lincoln High next year," Chase called over his shoulder. The last thing I wanted to talk about was high school.

"Yeah, what's so great about it?" I asked absently. My mind was mostly on Santiago and what Ava had found.

"We have the best football and basketball teams in the county. Our dances are awesome. You get to go on an amazing ski trip every year. And the teachers are pretty good too, if you're into classes and stuff."

"Sounds wonderful," I said as we pulled into the mall's parking lot and my stomach dropped into the pit of my stomach. Ava and I climbed out, but the guys stayed behind. "Be back here in thirty minutes," Ava ordered and I wondered what kind of spell this girl could put on people to make them do anything she wanted.

Ava grabbed my arm and led me to the mall's entrance. "He's in the food court. He's been going there almost every day."

I remembered Sherry telling me she had seen him there also. "Now, Bex," Ava said in a motherly tone. "Don't flip out or anything. Just stay calm and act like you don't really care. If he's eating something, dump it over his head. If you get some on the girl, that's a bonus."

I had no intentions of dumping anything over anyone's head, but I wanted to know what was going on.

As we neared the food court, Ava grabbed my hand and pulled me behind a tall fountain. "There."

I looked in the direction where she pointed. Sure enough, there was Santiago, sitting with a very beautiful girl, drinking blue slushies. *Our* blue slushies. They seemed to just be talking. That was until Santiago reached over and grabbed the girl's hand. A lump rose in my throat but I promised myself that I wouldn't cry in the middle of the mall, not over a two-timing boy. It was one thing to hear about him out with another girl, but actually seeing it was one hundred times worse.

"What are you waiting for?" Ava snapped. "Get over there and go off on him. And he's drinking a blue slushie. That's perfect for dumping!"

But I couldn't. At that moment I wasn't angry. I was hurt, and I wanted to burst into tears. "No, let's get out of here."

"What? You're not going to do anything?"

"Not right now. I just needed to see it with my own eyes. I want to go now."

Ava looked sincerely disappointed. She apparently had been looking forward to a great show of Santiago getting embarrassed in the middle of the food court.

When Chase dropped me off at home, Ava walked me to the door. "I'm really sorry, Bex. I was hoping not to find anything, but unfortunately, I did."

I glared at her. "You're sorry? You looked mighty happy to me."

Ava stepped back, looking confused, and I was very aware that I was taking my anger at Santiago out on her.

"Happy? Bex, I didn't want to find Santiago cheating on you. I just did what you asked me to. I was hoping to see you give him what he deserved. I'm really sorry about this."

I could tell from her eyes that she was sorry. "Thanks, Ava. I know you were only trying to help, and I shouldn't be taking my anger out on you."

"It's all right. See you tomorrow. We start setting the gym up for graduation."

"Yeah, see you tomorrow."

The first time Santiago called me that night I didn't answer. The second time . . . well, let's just say the second time wasn't so pretty.

"What do you want?" I demanded.

"H-hey, Bex. You all right?"

"Am I all right? Am I all right? What kind of question is that? Of course I'm not all right you lying, jerky traitor!"

"What's wrong with you?" Santiago yelled.

"You're what's wrong with me!"

"You're just like my mom, flying off the handle for no good reason. *Women*!"

"Oh, I have a reason, buddy. I have a *reason*." With that I hung up the phone. I made up my mind then and there. I wasn't just going to break up with Santiago. I was going to make his life miserable.

Chapter 8

Don't get mad, get evil!

—feeling furious :<

Journal Entry #21

Aunt Alice,

I'm actually kind of embarrassed to be telling you this, but because I consider you a friend as well as my aunt, and I trust you to keep this a secret, I'll spill.

Santiago is cheating on me. Please don't tell Aunt Jeanie because I'm not even allowed to be dating. Anyway, I was hurt, extremely hurt when I found out. Santiago and I have been good friends since we were little kids and I trusted him. Then my hurt turned to anger, hot burning anger and I felt like I just had to get him back for hurting me. I know you don't need to take advice from your fourteen-year-old niece, and I hope you're never in this situation, but if you are, whatever you do, don't do this. Let's just say things got a little out of control . . .

I should have known better than to tell Lily-Rose Johnston anything that would make her angry. I know her. She's a ticking time bomb wrapped in a cute tiny package. But she, Marishca, and Chirpy are my best friends, and I just had to tell them about Santiago and the girl at the mall.

We were in PE, sitting in the bleachers waiting for our turn to play volleyball when I dropped the news.

"Oh, no, Bex. I'm so sorry," Marishca said, looking as if she were going to cry.

Chirpy turned bright red. "I can't believe Santiago. That rat!"

Lily-Rose stood with her tiny fists clenched. "I told you. We should have gotten them when I wanted to. It's not too late. We know where he lives."

Normally, I would calm Lily-Rose down when she got like this, but this time, I was with her. I just wanted to hurt Santiago and make him feel the way I felt.

Just then, Coach O'Connell called us to the court for our turn to play so we didn't have time to brainstorm revenge ideas.

Before I knew it, Coach was blowing the whistle for us to hit the locker room. As I put the volleyball back into the bin of balls, the boys came in from the football field all hot and sweaty.

"Hey, Lily-Rose," Maverick called as he passed.

"Don't you 'Hey, Lily-Rose me'!" she snapped with her hands on her hips. I wondered why she was mad at Maverick and he looked just as confused as I did, but I didn't have much time to think about that because Santiago walked in not far behind him.

All the anger and rage I had been holding in came to a boiling point. I grabbed a ball from the large bin which held a variety of sports balls and hurled a soccer ball at Santiago's head.

He looked at me with his mouth and eyes wide open, but he didn't have time to say anything.

Because they're the best friends I could ever ask for and they always had my back, the Tribe grabbed balls and pelted Santiago with them as he ran yelling into the boys' locker room.

"Girls! Knock it off and pick up those balls!" Coach O'Connell shouted at us. By then the entire gym had erupted into laughter and another ball fight had broken out. Everyone was grabbing balls and hurtling them at each other just for the fun of it.

Coach had to blow her whistle ten times before the balls stopped flying. "Who started this?" she demanded as discarded balls rolled across the gym floor.

No one said anything. Coach O'Connell put her hands on her hips. "Speak now or you will all have detention for an entire week."

I couldn't let everyone get detention because of me. Either way I would be in trouble. "It was me, Coach."

She smirked. "I should have known, Carter. You couldn't let the year come to an end without one last detention, huh? See me tomorrow before school. I'll have something for you to do."

I groaned. Coach O'Connell gave the worst detentions because she never gave them after school, she only did them in the morning, which meant I would have to get up super early.

Hopefully this would be the last detention of my middle school career.

After school, the girls and I headed for Mrs. Diaz's room for our Graduation Committee meeting. As we rounded a corner, Santiago stepped in front of us looking very un-Santiago-like. As a matter of fact he looked downright furious. I'd never seen him look that way.

"What was that all about?" he demanded, looking at each of us.

Lily-Rose stepped forward. "You know very well what that was about, and you know you deserved it!"

"Yeah!" Marishca and Chirpy agreed.

"What? Did you all lose your minds on the same day?" Santiago asked. "I know you guys can be crazy but—"

"You haven't seen crazy yet," Lily-Rose warned.

Santiago took a step back. "Oh, I know what your crazy is like, but what did I ever do to you?"

"You know, Santiago," Marishca yelled. "Stop playing stupeed."

He rolled his eyes and sighed. "Let me talk to Bex, please."

The girls looked at me, and I nodded, indicating that I would be all right.

"What do we need to talk about?" I asked.

"What do we need t—Bex, what was that in PE? You totally humiliated me, and volleyballs hurt."

I lost it. "Volleyballs hurt? I humiliated *you*? How do you think I feel? And Ava knows, so pretty soon the whole school is going to know. You're making me look like some kind of loser." I was so angry I wanted to reach into his chest, pull out his little cheating heart, and squash it.

"Bex, what are you talking about? What do you think I've done?"

"It's not what I *think*. I saw it with my own eyes. How could you do that to me?" I stomped away because I felt tears welling up in my eyes, and I refused to cry in front of him.

"Bex, come on," Santiago called after me. "I can't deal with this right now." He said some other things, but I wasn't listening. I had stepped into Mrs. Diaz's classroom, and the committee was in the middle of a heated debate.

"Streamers are so tacky," Ava M. was saying.

"And balloons?" Ava T. added. "This is our eighth-grade graduation, not some little kid's birthday party."

Mrs. Diaz had pictures of decorating examples displayed on the projector. The first thing that caught my eye was a beautiful balloon arch with the class year in the middle.

"That would look great in front of the stage," I commented, sucking in my tears as quickly as possible.

"That's what we all think," Kenny said. "Except for *them*."

I knew *them* meant the Avas. Of course they were opposed to anything everyone else liked.

"I also like those columns made out of balloons," Chirpy said. Kenny wrote that on the board, and Ava huffed.

"Those streamers would look really nice going across the front of the stage," Mrs. Diaz commented.

Ava G. couldn't stand the fact that not even the teacher was on her side. "I thought we were supposed to be making the suggestions."

Mrs. Diaz gave her the Teacher Look. "You are, but I'm certainly free to share my opinions, am I not, Ms. Groves?"

Ava turned red and scowled. Kenny added gold stars that we could use to decorate the curtains, a good luck banner, and flowers to our list.

"Now," Mrs. Diaz said, "you need to price these things and make sure they're in the eighth-grade class budget, and then we'll purchase them."

We went to the laptop carts and grabbed computers to find the best pricing for the items. While some of us worked, the Avas kept suggesting ridiculous things like ice sculptures and a butterfly release.

"You want to release a thousand butterflies in that auditorium? Gross," Paisley Thomas remarked.

Ava G. glared her evil green eyes at her. "That would happen outside after the ceremony, idiot."

"Ms. Groves," Mrs. Diaz warned, "if you continue to be disrespectful, you'll be asked to leave."

"What about a dove release?" Ava T. said. That was even dumber than the butterfly idea.

"That would be much too expensive. Besides, it will be dark out," Mrs. Diaz replied, shooting down the idea. The Avas got to work looking for other ideas, desperate to have something they wanted as part of the décor.

"Chandeliers for the stage!"

"Gold trees lining the aisles."

"Rose petals sprinkled across the stage." Sure, so we can all slip and break our necks, I thought, but everyone was ignoring them anyway.

"What about a lighted monogram with our school's initials reflecting off the curtains," Ava G. suggested as we packed to leave.

"That's actually not a bad idea," Mrs. Diaz said and Ava looked extremely satisfied that one of her suggestions had been taken seriously.

Ava caught up with me as my friends and I walked to the front of the school. I thought she was going to say something about the ceremony decorations, but she didn't. "I heard about the ball thing in PE. That was okay, but you've got to get him back better than that."

I knew I did, but I couldn't think of a way that didn't involve me and my friends going to jail. "How?"

"Think about it. Do something meaningful. You say blue slushies were your favorite thing, so get him back with that."

I knew this conversation was headed for a very, very bad place, but I was still so angry that I didn't stop it.

Ava put her arm around me. "Leave it to me. I'll plan everything." I should have known better.

That night we met at Jeeves' house to help him work on his final project and prepare for his test. He had finally gotten it through his thick skull that William Shakespeare was none of the answers.

Mr. Chin had also given him the assignment of making a moving diorama from one of the scenes from a classic piece of literature. His dining room table was littered with markers, colored pencils, glue, paint, construction paper, and many other supplies.

Jeeves had chosen to do his diorama on "The Hobbit," and we would have a dragon sliding back and forth on a piece of wire.

We all got to work on it. Santiago once again was a no-show, but I was happy about that because I didn't want to see him.

While the boys were setting some things out on the patio to dry, I filled the girls in on Ava's plan, and they were all in. Operation Get-Back-At-Cruddy-Two-Timer was under way.

Chapter 9

Operation Get-Back-At-Cruddy-
Two-Timer

—feeling regretful ☹

Journal Entry #22

I think I've made the biggest mistake ever. A wise friend once told me not to jump to conclusions, but could I listen? No! Of course not. I can be such a jerk sometimes.

The Tribe and I were waiting in front of the skating rink for Ava, ready to pull off our brilliant plan. Chase's yellow Mustang pulled up, and Ava hopped out. She motioned for us to come toward the trunk.

She opened it and inside was a cooler filled with large pitchers of blue slushie. "Helga spent all day making these," Ava said, handing a container to each of us. Danny climbed out of the car, looking extremely bored.

"See you in a few," Ava said to Chase as he pulled off. "Danny, go get your friends and do what I said," Ava said bossily. Danny groaned and disappeared inside.

"What do they have to do?" Lily-Rose asked.

"They're going to block off the area. We don't want anyone out there but Santiago. Now come on before this stuff melts."

We followed her inside and headed straight for the stairs. The second floor of the skating rink was filled with game rooms and a couple of places to eat. Ava led us outside to the balcony area.

Two kids from our school were there making out. They jumped when they saw us. "Out of here," Ava ordered and they rushed inside.

Ava's phone chirped, and she pulled it from her back pocket. "Ava T. says he's on the way out."

"What are you talking about?" I asked.

"Santiago thinks there's a kid standing out here who wants to buy one of his hall passes." Ava lifted her pitcher and set it on the railing. "Get ready, girls."

I had mixed feelings about this. Yes, I wanted to get back at Santiago, but something inside of me was screaming that this was just wrong. Very wrong.

Ava must have read the expression on my face. "Bex, don't you dare feel sorry about this. He broke your heart. He deserves this and much, much more. This is for girls everywhere!" she yelled with her fist in the air. I got the feeling she was taking her anger at Grayson out on Santiago.

"Zere he eez," Marishca announced.

"Now!" Ava ordered.

We all tipped our pitchers over the railing and globs and globs of blue slushie fell on Santiago. I heard a girl scream and then realized someone else was standing beside him. It must have been the girl he was cheating on me with.

Santiago wiped the slushie from his eyes and looked up. "Bex! What's wrong with you? What did you do that for?"

I wanted to yell at him and tell him this was all his fault, but I couldn't. I felt bad about what we had done. We had gone way too far, and I wished we could take it back.

I don't know what happened to Santiago after that because he and the girl disappeared. The other girls felt proud about what had happened, but I didn't. Santiago and I didn't speak again until the night of the graduation ceremony. On top of that, because of the mess we made, we were all banned from the skating rink for an entire year.

That night I moped around the house feeling very guilty about what I had done. What if someone had dumped tons of slushie on me? How would I feel? I would have been humiliated. And that poor girl. What if she had no idea that she was the other woman? She could have been an innocent victim in all of this.

I lay on my bedroom floor staring at the ceiling. I wanted to call Santiago and tell him how sorry I was, but I knew he probably didn't want to talk to me. I wouldn't have wanted to talk to me.

The doorbell rang, and I wondered who had come over. I prayed it wasn't Mrs. Groves and Ava because I didn't feel like talking about what had happened at the skating rink. I wanted to forget it. After a few moments there was a knock on my bedroom door.

Hmm. That was different. Who actually had the good manners to knock before barging into my room?

"Bex? Are you in here?"

I hopped up and ran for the door. "Aunt Alice!" I flung the door open and wrapped my arms around her.

"How are you?"

"Okay," I lied. I was not okay at all.

Aunt Alice closed the door behind her and pointed to my bed. "What's wrong?"

Aunt Alice was almost like a big sister to me. She was my mom's and Aunt Jeanie's baby sister and the complete opposite of Aunt Jeanie. She had long, curly, light brown hair and hazel eyes that always twinkled. We had a lot in common, mainly our love of writing. Aunt Alice was a photojournalist who traveled all over the world. Sometimes she was gone for weeks at a time and I really missed her. Even though she was a grownup, she was one of my best friends. I could tell her *almost* anything.

We sat side by side on my bed. "What's going on?" she asked.

I shrugged. "Not much. Just getting ready for graduation and . . ."

Her eyes seemed to smile at me, and I couldn't hold my emotions in any longer. Everything I had been holding inside came out and I burst like a dam.

"Aunt Alice, I'm really, really stressed out about high school and losing my friends and having to meet new people and then there's this thing with Ava. We have to pretend to be friends so we don't have to spend the summer shoveling cow poop, and I'm so confused about her because sometimes she can be nice, and sometimes I want to strangle her. Then there's Santiago . . . I really like him a lot, but he's interested in another girl, but he doesn't want to tell me so he's been sneaking around with her, and it makes me feel so bad and . . . my friends and I did a really bad thing to them, and I wish I could take it back. It was horrible."

Aunt Alice stared at me wide-eyed. "Well, that is a lot of stuff going on. I know about the Santiago thing. That's why I wanted to talk to you."

My jaw dropped. "How do you know about Santiago?"

"His mother called Jeanie, and Jeanie called me and gave me an earful. Once she was done yelling at me, I told her that I would come over and talk to you."

"Why would she be mad at you?" I asked. "You had nothing to do with what happened." Honestly, trying to understand Aunt Jeanie could be like trying to solve the sphinx's riddle. I just didn't get her sometimes.

"Well, a while ago she and I had an argument about whether or not you were ready to have a boyfriend. She had to let me know that she was right about you being too immature to deal with that right now. She was also a little hurt that you were dating, if you can call it that, Santiago behind her back. She thinks I knew about it."

"But you didn't."

"That's what I've been trying to tell her, but she doesn't believe it. Doesn't matter anyway. She's always mad at me for some reason or another. Anyway, I have to agree with her about you not being ready."

Ouch.

"Bex, when you have a problem with someone, talk to him or her. Usually, there's a good reason for people to be acting the way they've acted. Take poor Santiago for instance. His mother was very upset about what happened because he's already dealing with some other things."

"Like what?" I asked.

"I'm not sure."

"Well, why didn't he tell me if he was going through something?" I asked, although I should have picked up on the clues from his change in personality. I noticed something was different, but Aunt Alice was right. I had never taken the time to ask if something was bothering him.

Aunt Alice smiled at me. "I'm sure if you ask him he'll tell you. And as for Ava, I'm not trying to justify her behavior over the years, but have you ever thought about why she acts the way she does?"

I shook my head. Usually people were mean because other people had been mean to them or something terrible had happened in their lives. That wasn't Ava. Her life was perfect. I had no idea what made mean girls mean, but I didn't think there was any excuse for it.

Aunt Alice lay in my bed and we talked late into the night about boys, high school, and friendship. Aunt Alice told me she didn't keep in contact with any of her friends from high school anymore, and that made me sad. I silently vowed that would never happen to the Tribe. We would be friends forever.

Aunt Jeanie finally peeked her head in and asked Aunt Alice if she were planning on spending the night or what. There was something unfriendly in the way she asked it, and I detected a little jealousy. She and I never had long conversations like that. I didn't like making Aunt Jeanie feel bad, but Aunt Alice was so much easier to talk to than she was.

Aunt Alice pulled herself up from the bed. "Don't worry, Jeanie, I'm leaving." She looked at me. "You're still keeping that journal, right? It's part of our deal."

"Yep," I replied. "I can't wait for you to read it."

She winked at me. "I can't wait for our trip. I know you'll make it."

As Aunt Alice left, Aunt Jeanie raised her eyebrow at me. "We'll talk in the morning, Bex."

I shuddered. I knew some type of punishment was coming for what I had done to Santiago, and I very much deserved it.

Chapter 10

And the award for best actress goes to . . .

—feeling exhausted ☹

Journal Entry # 23

Pretending to be friends with someone is a lot of work. I don't get how some people do it. If it weren't for this trip to Australia or the threat of spending my ENTIRE summer on a farm with Ava, I wouldn't even bother. And trust me when I tell you that Ava isn't making it easy. She's doing her best to make sure I earn this trip to Australia.

Ava and I didn't feel we had her mother and my aunt convinced enough to think we had honestly become best friends. Ava suggested that I come over to her house and hang out one afternoon. I didn't really want to. As a matter of fact there were a million other things I'd rather be doing, but best friends hung out at each other's houses, so I had to play the part.

When Aunt Jeanie dropped me off at the Groves', I rang their doorbell and prayed that I would make it through this afternoon. It wasn't me that I was worried about. I was afraid that Ava would blow our cover. I never knew which Ava I was going to get, the mean one or the semi-mean one. Any argument we ever had was entirely her fault so I hoped that Ava would behave herself.

Mrs. Groves opened the door. Her face lit up. "I'm so happy to see you girls spending time together. Ava's in her bedroom. Go right on up."

When I reached the top of the staircase, I heard several voices drifting from Ava's room. I got a queasy feeling in my stomach. I had been under the impression that it was going to be just the two of us. For some reason, Ava was usually nicer to me when no one else was around.

I swallowed hard and knocked on her door. Unlike her, I wasn't rude enough to just barge into someone's bedroom, even though she'd done it to me more than once.

"Shh," someone hissed and the voices fell silent. A few seconds later, the door opened and Ava poked her head out. "Oh, Bex. You've made it." She stepped away from the door and I stepped inside. I wanted to go home immediately once I realized the voices belonged to Ava T. and Ava M. I should have known.

This was totally unfair! Three against one. If I had known the other Avas were going to be there, I would have invited my friends, and we would have had them outnumbered.

The other Avas were perched on Ava G.'s all-white canopy bed looking at something on her laptop.

"Hey, Bex, nice outfit," Ava T. said, looking me up and down. I knew she was being sarcastic, and I didn't care. So I wasn't dressed my best that day. I was wearing a pair of denim shorts and a plain white T-shirt. I didn't see anything wrong with that.

"You're just in time," Ava M. said. "We needed an even number."

So that's why Ava had invited me over. They needed an even number of people for something. "An even number for what?" I asked skeptically.

"Our hair battle," Ava G. announced. "We're doing teams this time, and Helga will be the judge." Helga was the Groves' housekeeper. "Sarah Roberts is usually our fourth, but she's grounded."

"That's great because I had nothing better to do than to be your last-minute substitution for whatever stupid thing you guys have going on," I said.

The three girls stared at me. Ava G. rolled her eyes. "Duh, Bex. That's why I called you."

I groaned. "What exactly is a hair battle?" I asked, knowing that I'd rather be doing anything else at that moment.

"We each style someone else's hair and then we ask Helga to pick her favorite style. Of course we won't tell her who styled whom, even though Helga would be completely impartial."

Yeah right, I thought to myself.

"I'm . . . really not that good at hair and besides, that sounds extremely boring. Why don't we go in the Jacuzzi instead?"

Ava G. frowned at me. "Do you have any idea how hot it is? Only a lunatic would get in a Jacuzzi right now."

I sat in Ava's desk chair and folded my arms across my chest. "Well, I'm not doing your stupid hair battle."

Ava glared at me, and the other Avas stood beside her glaring equally as hard. Who did they think they were? I wasn't afraid of them.

Ava M. curled her upper lip. "If she won't cooperate, Ava, just tell your mom. Let her know this friendship thing isn't working. I hope you like working on a farm, Bex."

"Newsflash, stupid. If Ava does that she'll be landing her butt on that farm too," I snapped.

Ava G. thought for a moment. "Maybe not. Not if I go downstairs and tell my mother that I'm trying so hard," she said in a fake whiny voice. "I invited you over and planned this awesome activity for us, but you won't even meet me halfway. She'll feel so sorry for me and let me go to Camp Pointe and you will be on that farm all by yourself."

I was calling her bluff. "Fine. Go ahead. Tell her."

Ava stormed over to the door and yanked it open. "Oh, Mother!"

I thought for a moment. There was no way Mrs. Groves would believe me over her precious daughter. If I was going to be stuck on that farm, Ava would be too. If she was going to Camp Pointe, I was going to Australia.

"Okay, okay," I muttered. How hard would a hair battle really be? It's not like I really cared about winning. All I had to do was brush someone's hair up into a ponytail and shove some bows in it. Voila!

Ava closed her door. "Good. Let's begin. Ladies, choose your models."

"I want Bex!" all the girls said at the same time.

"Wait a minute. Why does everyone want to do my hair?" I asked suspiciously.

"Because," Ava T. said, "hair battles are a chance to go crazy and do styles you wouldn't normally do, you know, high-fashion stuff. We can do so much with that big fuzz ball of yours."

I bit my tongue at her fuzz ball comment, and all I knew about high fashion was that it usually meant weird.

"Bex is my best friend so I get to style her," Ava G. said. With that, the issue was closed.

I had to do Ava M.'s hair. Ava M. had to do Ava T.'s and Ava T. had to do Ava G.'s. I know, I know that sounds really confusing and really, who cares? Was this really what these girls did for fun?

I worked on Ava M.'s hair first because Ava G. said she wanted to do my hair last. Ava M. had fine light blonde hair that fell almost to her waist. I took a curling iron and began to make spiral curls. After a while I got kind of tired of doing that, realizing that it was going to take me forever, so I started to make them bigger. Ava G. kept looking over and giving my work the stink-eye, but I couldn't have cared less.

Once I was done making mismatched curls, I made a braid going across the front of her head. I had seen a lot of people wearing their hair like that lately, and I thought it was cute. I went through Ava's drawers, which were jam-packed with accessories, and found a pretty silver butterfly clip. I stuck it into Ava M.'s hair, but I may have done it a little too hard.

She winced. "Ow, Bex! Are you trying to stab me in the brain?"

"Sorry," I said, even though I really wasn't.

After that, it was time for me to sit for Ava to do my hair. She wouldn't let me look in any mirrors or tell me what she was doing. This scared me because I did not trust Ava at all.

It seemed to take forever as she braided, twisted, curled, and poked, but finally she was done. The other Avas gathered around.

"Wow, Ava. This isn't going to even be a contest," Ava M. said.

"Yeah," Ava T. chirped in. "I've never seen Bex look better."

I wasn't stupid, and I noticed the way they were both holding in giggles. Ava T. and Ava M. would not win any

Academy Awards. From the strange things I felt hanging from my head, I knew I looked terrible.

Before I knew it, Ava G. had snapped a picture of me with her phone and was yelling for Helga to come judge.

I had to look at myself, so I turned and headed for the mirror. Ava G. grabbed my arm. "Wait, Bex, we have to do the line up for Helga."

The four of us stood side by side and waited for Helga. A short, stocky woman with white-blond hair pulled up in a neat bun stepped cautiously into Ava's room. I was sure she had more important things to do other than judging this stupid contest.

Helga's eyes glossed across the four of us. "Uh . . . I–I have to go with number three," she said, pointing at me.

Ava G. squealed and jumped up and down while the other Avas groaned and headed for the mirrors. Did they really think Ava G. was *not* going to win?

Ava pulled her phone from her jeans pocket. "I have to share this."

I dashed over to her mirror, practically shoving the other Avas aside. My stomach dropped when I saw myself. My suspicions had been well founded. I looked like some sort of psychedelic jellyfish. Most of my hair was twisted into messy, lumpy braids which Ava had intertwined with different color ribbons. Then she'd had the audacity to shove a big pink bow on the top of my head. My eleven-year-old cousins, who had yet to realize they were too old for bows, wouldn't have been caught dead in such a babyish bow, and they were the bow-wearing queens.

"Very avant-garde, huh?" Ava G. asked, still looking at her phone.

"I don't know what that means, but if it means utter abomination, yes!"

The Avas all broke into giggles. "Look!" Ava G. shouted excitedly as she looked at her phone. "It's already got a hundred likes."

I began to pull the braids out of my hair. "Likes?" I asked as a dreadful feeling came over me.

"Oh, I shared it on my Snap-A-Gram page. I have thousands of followers."

"What?" I screamed. "How could you?" But I knew how she could. She was an evil conniving little vermin. "Delete it."

"Nope," she said simply, plopping down on her bed.

My face burned, and I was seething. I had to get her back. I had to make her pay for humiliating me. I knew the next day at school that picture was all anyone would be talking about. Once you put something out on the Internet, it was out there forever.

When you're playing with evil, sometimes you had to get evil. I got an especially evil idea.

"If we're done, I'm going to text my aunt to come get me," I said calmly. The girls looked shocked at my sudden change in demeanor. Ava even looked disappointed. She had wanted me to flip out on her.

But I did more than text Aunt Jeanie. I went on my Snap-A-Gram page (even though I didn't have nearly as many followers) and posted this:

Guess what popular girl has gotten her heart stomped on by an older guy. He cheated on her and dumped her right at her birthday party! This girl! Smile, Ava.

Then I took a quick picture of her and posted it. I was so angry, it seemed like a good idea at the time. "I'll wait for my Aunt Jeanie on the porch."

I had just hit the bottom of the staircase when I heard something that sounded like a cat being tortured. "Beeeeeeeeeex!"

Mission accomplished.

Chapter 11

A Picture's Worth A Thousand Words

#SoOverCeremonyPlanning

The next day at school was murder. I had already prepared myself for the laughs and stares that were coming my way as a result of Ava's Snap-A-Gram post.

"Hey, Bex. What happened to the new do?" Kristen Lee asked as she passed me. "It was actually an improvement." Kristen was probably the second meanest girl in school, although sometimes I thought she and Ava might be neck and neck.

Several idiots shouted names at me like Medusa and Octo-Bex. What were these kids? Five? Maybe I was ready for high school. Surely the kids there weren't this immature.

I found my friends waiting for me by my locker. "Yikes. We saw the picture," Chirpy said. "That was brutal."

"Yeah, it was, but . . ." Marishca began, then looked away.

"Yeah, but what?" I asked.

"What you did to her was a lot worse."

Chirpy and Lily-Rose nodded in agreement. "But," Lily-Rose added quickly, "I approve because Ava totally deserved it. She started the whole thing."

"Yeah," I reminded myself, since I was starting to feel a little guilty. "She did. I just finished it."

"Ahem," said someone from behind me. I turned to face Ava M. whose hair was now straight again.

"What?" I asked.

"Ava G. would like to have a quick meeting with you. She's in the girls' bathroom at the end of the hall, last stall."

I'd had enough of meeting Ava in bathrooms. I looked at my friends. Marishca bit her bottom lip. "I suppose you're going to have to face her sooner or later. Want us to come?"

"No, I can handle it. See you guys later." I left my friends and headed for the girls' room. I poked my head in, hoping someone else would be inside in case Ava tried to kill me, but the bathroom was empty.

"Ava?" I called.

"Yeah," she answered quietly. I could tell from the tremble in her voice that she was crying.

I passed the row of sinks and mirrors and stood in front of her stall. "You're not going to do this, Ava. You don't get to cry and make me feel guilty when you started the whole thing."

She blew her nose. "What you did to me was so much worse. Everybody's laughing at me. I told you that in confidence. I trusted you. I'm not the girl who gets dumped—I'm the girl who does the dumping. You've ruined my reputation."

I tried to hold my resolve and not fold underneath the strain of her tears and sob story, but I caved. I felt bad because Ava had told me about Grayson in confidence, and in my anger and desire for revenge, I wanted to get back at her and teach her a lesson. I guess I had, but I didn't feel good about it.

Ava unlocked the stall and stepped out. "I deleted the picture."

"Thanks for that, but everyone had already seen and shared it."

She nodded solemnly. "Yeah, I know. I shouldn't have posted it in the first place."

"Why did you do that? We're supposed to be trying to get along."

Ava shrugged. "I forgot about that for a minute, I guess. I thought it would be funny."

"Okay, but can we try not being funny at the expense of other people?"

She gave me a half smile. "Are we cool?"

"Yeah. We're cool."

I should have known that "We're cool" only meant "We're cool for now" to Ava.

Friday's Graduation Committee meeting was super important because we would be putting together the slide show for our ceremony.

Mrs. Diaz had given us very strict instructions before the meeting began. "We want all the clubs, teams, and groups to be represented. Of course every student won't be pictured, but try to get as many class and group shots as possible. Think about the major events we've had this year and include those too."

Roman Belle, the editor of the yearbook, had sent us all the pictures the yearbook staff had taken throughout the year so we could go through them and decide which to include in the slide show.

"Not to fear," Ava announced. "We took care of the slide show a while ago."

Everyone groaned. We didn't even have to see the slide show to know it would be Ava-centric.

Kenny hooked a laptop up to the projector at the front of the room. "Okay, let us see it," he said with absolutely no enthusiasm. Ava T. handed him a flash drive. A moment later our ears were assaulted by the song "Platinum Girl."

Across the screen flashed:

1. A picture of the cheerleading squad

2. A picture of the Avas posing at a basketball game

3. A picture of Ava G. dancing at one of her parties

4. A picture of the cheerleaders' bake sale

5. A picture of the basketball team

6. A picture of the science club

7. A picture of Ava and her friends during lunch

8. A picture of Ava walking down the runway at the school's fashion show

9. A blurry out-of-focus picture of the band

Kenny cut the slide show off. We didn't need to see any more to know where things were going.

"What was that?" Chirpy demanded. "This is supposed to be the eighth-grade slide show, not the Ava Show."

Ava looked confused because in her mind the world was the Ava Show. "People want to look at pretty things. I'm just giving them what they want. Who wants to look at pictures of the chess club? Have you seen those guys?"

The room erupted into shouting and arguing, the loudest voice belonging to a boy named Troy who was in the chess club. We got so loud that Mrs. Diaz rushed into the room. "What is going on?" she asked, frowning.

"Ava G. wants the whole slide show to be about her," Kenny said.

Ava flipped her hair at him. "It's not just about us. We added pictures of the cutest guys too."

Mrs. Diaz was quiet for a moment. "Maybe this was a bad idea. I think the teachers should—"

"No!" we all shouted. We didn't want the teachers to put together the slide show for us.

"We can handle it, Mrs. Diaz," I assured her.

She glanced across the room. "I hope so. Remember, all groups are to be included."

She went back into her office, and we got to work.

"The slide show gets better," Ava M. said. "Just watch another minute."

Before anyone could object, she had turned it on again and it picked up from where it had left off.

10. A picture of the cheerleading squad at the state competition

11. A picture of Ava G.'s cat, Frisky (Seriously?)

12. Then there was THE PICTURE—the picture Ava had taken of me after the hair battle. The one she said she was sorry for posting on Snap-A-Gram, yet here she was, displaying it for all to see.

The room fell silent. A few kids snickered, but Lily-Rose shot them a look and they stopped.

"Really, Ava?" Kenny asked as he cut the slide show off.

Ava smirked at me. "I have no idea how that picture got in there. That must have been a mistake." Then she took her seat, trying to look as innocent as possible.

I should have seen this coming, but I hadn't because I didn't have the evil brain Ava had. I should have seen through her act in the bathroom. She wasn't apologetic at all. The whole time she had been planning to get back at me even though she had started it.

Chirpy patted my shoulder, but it was fine. I was happy Ava's little stunt hadn't gotten the reaction she was probably expecting. Either all the kids in the room had already seen the picture and gotten their laughs out or they were over Ava and her antics.

"Let's move on," Chirpy said.

While the slide show played, someone had made a list of all the groups in the school, and we checked them off as we added their picture to the slide show. Ava kept insisting that the cheerleaders get more pictures because they were the most popular group and everyone wanted to be a cheerleader.

"You get one picture, Buttercup, and that's it," Troy shouted forcefully. Ava withered just a bit. It was nice to see other people stand up to her.

Ava G. watched over Kenny's shoulder as he uploaded pictures. "Well, I have cheerleading, the Fashion Club, the Dance Committee, the Junior Honor Society, the Pep Squad, and the Dance Team. That's six pictures. I'll probably have more pictures than anyone else."

That's all she was worried about: how many pictures she would have in the slide show. The levels of her selfishness never ceased to amaze me.

Chapter 12
Lincoln High, Here We Come

#memories

Journal Entry #24

Our graduation ceremony was really nice, but it was bittersweet. I had gone to school with these kids for the past two years and some of them since the first grade. This was the last time we would all be together because a lot of kids would be going to different high schools. Those of us who were going on to Lincoln High would be mixed in with kids coming from other middle schools and well . . . let's just say things would never be the same.

After second period, we all gathered outside of Jeeves' Language Arts class as he waited for Mr. Chin to grade his projects. Even Santiago was there, though he wasn't speaking to anyone but Maverick. He wouldn't even look at me, which made me feel terrible. I couldn't blame him though.

After two minutes of waiting, Jeeves stepped into the hallway, looking dejected.

"Oh no, you failed!" Chirpy wailed.

Jeeves dropped the books he was carrying and started dancing. "Nope! I passed! By the skin of my teeth, but I passed."

We all cheered and patted him on the back. I was truly happy that my friend would be walking across the stage with us. Santiago and I made eye contact, then he dropped his gaze. "That's great, Jeeves. I knew you could do it. I've got to get to class. The bell's about to ring. See ya."

We watched him mope away. "It was really awful what you guys did to him," Maverick said. "The dude's having a hard enough time as it is."

"What do you know?" I demanded.

Maverick and Jeeves looked at each other. "Uh, nothing," Jeeves stammered. "I don't know what Maverick's talking about."

Maverick nodded. "Yeah, I don't know what I'm talking about either."

Jeeves backed away from us. "Man, let's get out of here before they dump slushies on our heads." Then the two of them scurried down the hallway like frightened mice.

I sighed and said good-bye to my friends before we were all late to class.

My family was making a huge deal about this graduation ceremony. I mean, you would have thought I was taking a voyage to Mars.

That was one thing about being the oldest kid and grandchild—everything was a big deal because I was the first to do it. By the time it was Ray's turn to graduate, they probably wouldn't care so much.

I slid on my plain black dress which Aunt Jeanie helped me dress up with a gold chain belt and gold accessories. It wasn't as cute as the green dress I had tried on, but I was happy with the way I looked.

Aunt Jeanie flat-ironed my hair which took *forever*, then we had to take family pictures which took even longer than *forever*.

"Aunt Jeanie, we're going to be late for the ceremony," I whined as she posed me for another picture with Francois.

This had been our tenth attempt at a photo because he kept making faces at me at the last minute.

"Okay, okay," she said as she hurriedly rushed the family out the door. This included Nana, Aunt Alice, and a very bored-looking Uncle Bob.

The students had been instructed to line up in front of the auditorium so that we could march down the aisles in alphabetical order. Since my last name was Carter, I was near the front.

My knees wobbled, and I prayed that I wouldn't trip in my heels, even though they weren't that high. Heels, a long gown, and a tassel bobbing in my face created a recipe for disaster.

I heard the music start from inside, and our assistant principal told us the procession was beginning.

I walked in slowly and steadily. I wanted to look around for my family in the crowd of people staring at us, but it was too much to look for them and concentrate on walking.

The auditorium was completely full and decorated beautifully (thanks to the awesome graduation committee!). The balloon arch was the best part, I thought as I crossed in front of it.

Breathing a sigh of relief that I had reached my destination without falling flat on my face, I took my seat on the stage facing the audience. The ceremony began and kind of went by in a blur. Mr. Radcliff gave a speech. He mostly talked about trying our best and that we had our whole lives ahead of us and we could do anything we wanted. Harold Kline, who was our class president, also gave a speech. We sang our song, which turned out to be the perfect choice. Each student was called to get his or her diploma. Then came the slide show, which made most of us cry.

After the ceremony, I took loads of pictures with my friends. At one point, Santiago walked up to me. He looked a little happier than usual, but his expression fell when he saw me. "Hey."

"Hey," I said. There was a long awkward pause as kids and parents milled around us in the parking lot. "Everything turned out nice, huh?"

"Yeah, it did. Uh, your aunt invited my family over for dinner at your house so I guess I'll see you there."

Aunt Jeanie had arranged for caterers to bring food to the house instead of us going to a restaurant because she insisted it would be more intimate. I had no idea she had invited Santiago and his family, and I wished she would have at least given me a heads up.

"See you there," I said as he walked away.

"Bex, are you ready?" Aunt Jeanie called.

I nodded and walked toward her. "Why did you have to invite Santiago to our house?"

She grabbed my arm. "Bex, it's the least I could do after you dumped all that goo on the poor boy. Now come. I want to get one more picture of you and Francois."

Dinner was nice at Aunt Jeanie's. We all sat around the long dining room table, and because it was my day, I didn't have to sit at the kids' table. Santiago and I sat side by side but didn't say one word to each other.

While the caterers prepared to serve dessert, I turned to Santiago. "I can't take it anymore. Can you please say something to me? Even if it's yelling."

He took a deep breath. "Can we go outside and talk?"

"Sure." We excused ourselves from the table and headed for the patio. We took a seat next to each other on lawn chairs. "What's up?"

"Bex, there's been some stuff going on that I haven't told you about. Mostly, I guess because I was afraid to say it."

Here it was. "I already know. You want to dump me for that other girl."

Santiago took my hand. "That other girl is my cousin."

"What? Your cousin?"

"Yeah, she's my mom's sister's daughter—"

"I know what a cousin is, but you were holding hands with her and drinking blue slushies with her. That's our thing."

Santiago turned my face toward his. "I was holding her hand because our family is going through a hard time, and blue slushies always make me feel better, so I thought they would cheer Isabella up."

Now I felt even worse than I already had. "What's going on with your family?"

"My *abuelo* died last week. He had gotten really sick, and then he took a turn for the worse."

My heart shuddered. "Santiago, I'm so sorry. Really, really sorry. Why didn't you tell me or any of us? We're your friends."

He shrugged. "Because every time I think about it I start to cry." Even then his eyes were welling with tears. "I didn't want to cry in front of you. I was going to tell you when I was ready to talk about it."

I knew how he must have been feeling. I remembered when my grandpa, Nana's husband, died, even though I was only a little girl. And if something ever happened to Nana . . . well, I couldn't even imagine it.

"Anyway," Santiago said, "*Abuelo* practically raised Isabella so she took it really hard. He was like a father to her."

I squeezed his hand harder. "I'm sorry," I repeated. "I'm super, super sorry about the slushie thing." I don't think I had ever felt like a bigger idiot.

"It's okay. I mean, it's not okay, but I should have been more straightforward with you and told you what was going on."

"And," I said. "I could have asked you instead of jumping to conclusions like I usually do."

Santiago looked at me and smiled, and I couldn't take my eyes off his adorable dimples. Then his smile dropped, and his dimples disappeared. "There's something else."

I braced myself, wondering what else he could possibly have to tell me. "Lay it on me."

"I've kind of been avoiding you because I've been trying to find a way to tell you this. My dad . . . his job is transferring him to Dallas, Texas. My family is going to be moving there this summer."

I didn't think my heart could drop any deeper into the pit of my stomach, but it did. "What?"

"Yeah, I didn't know how to tell you."

I let that awful news settle in for a second. Wow, his family really had been going through a lot, and I had spent the whole time being mad at him instead of being there for him. "What does that mean for us?"

He looked away from me then. "I don't know. We can still talk and video chat. I have family here, so we'll probably come and visit every so often."

"But it won't be the same," I said softly.

"No, it won't."

I realized that night that nothing in my life would ever be the same. I had been friends with Santiago since we were six, and I had never imagined him not being a part of my life. It just didn't seem real.

"I like you, Bex. I have for a long time. I've never come across a girl like you before, and I probably never will again. You're special. Don't forget it."

I leaned my head on his shoulder and cried. I cried for a few things. I cried for him losing his grandfather; for me losing him because I knew no matter what he said, once he moved that would be it. I cried out of fear that the Tribe would change, and I might lose my friends just like I was losing Santiago. I secretly wished that I could put them all in a box and make them stay with me forever.

Chapter 13
Real or Fake?

#totallybummed

Journal Entry #25

How many times must I have my heart broken? I'm only fourteen and my heart has been seriously broken twice. Unfortunately, Aunt Jeanie says it's only the beginning and I have a long way to go and that it doesn't get any easier. Sometimes I think Aunt Jeanie could use a class on giving a pep talk, but I do have to admire her honesty.

Santiago and I have decided to break it off as boyfriend and girlfriend. We promised that we would keep in contact and remain friends. I don't know. People say that all the time, but then don't do it. Hopefully it'll be different for us though.

I've been spending a lot of time with all my friends now that school's out and we've made a pact that we would be friends forever and always make time for each other no matter how often our lives changed. I believe we'll keep our promise to each other and that makes me feel a little better about high school.

As for Ava and our pact . . . let's just say life is full of surprises.

I was still grounded over the slushie incident, so I was sort of surprised when Aunt Jeanie burst into my room (without knocking of course) to make an announcement.

"The Groves and Uncle Bob and I are going to see a musical tonight, so Nana will be coming to babysit. Since you're grounded and Ava's grounded, you two can be grounded together. She's going to be sleeping over."

Ugh. Add sleepovers with Ava to a list of things I hate. Though Ava and I had had a few nice moments, I never knew which Ava I was going to get: the mean Ava or the semi-mean Ava.

"Yay!" I said as Aunt Jeanie looked at me strangely. "Clean up this pigsty of a room," she said, before closing the door.

The Groves came by at around 6:30, and Ava looked just as excited as I did, which was not very excited at all. I lay on my bed watching her blow up an air mattress. "I heard about you and Santiago. Sorry."

"Thanks," I said. I didn't talk much about our breakup because the wound was still fresh. Sometimes I would forget that he wasn't my boyfriend anymore.

"Look at the bright side," she said. "Now you can go to high school unattached. Single and ready to mingle. That's what I'm looking forward to. High school boys. Ones not like Grayson anyway."

I scowled at her. "Oh, really? What about Danny?"

She made a face at me. "Danny got to say he was my boyfriend for a few weeks, and I got his brother to drive me around. We're done."

"You're awful. Just when I think you might be okay, you do something like this. You used him and that's not right."

Ava glared at me. "Don't you judge me, Bex Carter. You have no idea how this stuff works. You are so *immature*."

I was about to give her a very big piece of my mind when I remembered something Aunt Alice had said. Maybe there's a reason Ava acts the way she does.

"Why are you so mean?"

She frowned and looked away. "Shut up, Bex."

"I really want to know."

"I'm not mean!"

"I don't get it. You're pretty. You're popular. You have parents who love you and give you everything you want. What do you get out of making other people miserable?"

She lay on her air mattress and closed her eyes.

"Take me and my friends for instance, we've never done anything to you, but you've been mean to us since we were little."

"Because you and your friends can be stupid and annoying sometimes."

That wasn't a good enough reason for me. "So why not just ignore us and leave us alone. Why talk to us at all?"

Ava shrugged.

"I think it's because you like to be in control. You're always ordering people around. In the meeting for the ceremony committee, when you weren't in control, it drove you crazy."

She still said nothing, but I knew I was getting somewhere. "I think your mom is just like Aunt Jeanie. They want to control every aspect of our lives—our hobbies, how we eat, how we look, how we dress. And since you don't have control over your life, you feel like you have to have control over something else. The funny thing is, I don't act the way you do."

Ava groaned. "Shut up! You think you're a psychologist now?"

"I think you can start over in high school. You don't have to be that way. The Avas and your other friends follow your lead. I'm sure you can be just as popular without being mean."

"Whatever, Bex" she said, rolling over, but I knew she was thinking about what I said. I didn't expect to change a bad girl overnight, but I could at least get her to think about it. Maybe if I kept reminding her, it would sink in.

Later that night, we actually painted each other's nails and told scary stories, something I'd never picture myself doing with Ava. She was actually decent. She didn't make one complaint or insult me the entire night.

Before we turned in Ava handed me a piece of folded paper.

"What's this?" I asked as I unfolded it.

"A receipt. Your new lamp should be here in a few days. It was a pain finding it, but I did. Sorry I broke the other one."

I didn't know what to say so I was glad when Ava kept talking. "I've been thinking . . . it's too much work fighting and hating each other all the time, so let's go into high school with a clean slate. I mean it this time."

I wanted to believe her, and I hoped she was being sincere. "Sounds good to me."

That's how my bogus, fake friend became my kind of, sort of real friend. We would probably never be besties, but friends was a start.

Life lessons from Bex:

If you have a problem with a friend, talk to him or her. Don't jump to conclusions or do something stupid when a simple conversation can solve your issues.

Life is full of surprises. I never thought I would be friends with Ava Groves, but she and I have done what we thought was impossible—learned to get along, and now we're on our way to having awesome summers. (No farm for us—woot!)

Also, life is all about change, so don't be afraid of it. Finally, never, I repeat, *never* dump blue (or any other color) slushie on someone's head. It's just wrong!

Stay tuned for Bex Carter #8 Coming Soon!

Made in the USA
Middletown, DE
15 May 2017